The Sufferers

The Sufferers
Stories and Polemics

Taha Hussein

Translated by Mona El-Zayyat

The American University in Cairo Press

English translation copyright © 1993 by
The American University in Cairo Press
113 Sharia Kasr el Aini
Cairo, Egypt

Published by arrangement with the Estate of Taha Hussein

Second paperback printing 1995

This translation based on the 1955 Dar al-Ma'arif edition of
al-Mu'adhdhabūna fi-l-ard.
Protected under the Berne Convention.

English renderings of quotations from the Quran are taken from
The Meaning of the Glorious Koran: An Explanatory Translation
by Marmaduke Pickthall, London: Alfred A. Knopf, 1930.

Dar el Kutub No. 2235/93
ISBN 977 424 313 7

Printed in Egypt at the Printshop of the American University in Cairo

Contents

Translator's Introduction

Taha Hussein was born on October 28, 1898, in al-Minya province, Upper Egypt, and grew up, the seventh of thirteen children, in a lower middle-class family. At a very early age he contracted a simple eye infection and, due to faulty treatment by an unskilled local practitioner, was unnecessarily blinded. His blindness caused him great anguish throughout his life.

He was placed in a *kuttab* (a school where children learned the Quran and reading and writing) and was later sent to al-Azhar, where he acquired a thorough knowledge of religion and Arabic literature in the traditional manner. However, he felt deep discontent with the narrow thinking and conservatism of his tutors, the shaykhs.

In 1908 he learned of the founding of a new, secular university as part of a national effort to promote education in Egypt under British occupation, and was very keen to enter it. He was blind, and he was poor, but, overcoming many obstacles, he was accepted in the Egyptian University. He later stated, in his trilogy *al-Ayyam* ('The Days') that "the doors of knowledge were from that day opened wide for him." He was the first graduate of this university to receive a Ph.D., with his thesis on the skeptic poet and philosopher Abu al-'Alaa' al-Ma'arri.

Again with much trouble, he was sent to study in France on the university's educational mission. His blindness caused him continuing pains, aggravated by a careless brother, presumably sent to take care of him. It was in France that he met his 'sweet voice,' Suzanne, who came to read to him since not all the references he needed were available in braille. She later became his wife, his mentor, advisor, assistant, mother to his children, great love, and best friend. In the first volume of his trilogy he states that since he first heard that 'sweet voice,' "anguish never again entered his heart." After his death she wrote *Ma'ak* ('With You'), published in Arabic, a touching remembrance of their life together.

Taha Hussein specialized in literature and classical studies and was, again, the first Egyptian, and the only member of the mission, to succeed in obtaining first his B.A. from Montpellier University, and then his Ph.D. from the Sorbonne. His doctoral dissertation, written in 1917, was on Ibn Khaldun, the fourteenth-century Arab historian, whom he showed to be the founder of sociology.

He had begun life blind and with only a grassroots education, living in a country then torn by economic and political strife and ruled by a king subservient to British occupation, but through his own will and craving for knowledge he grew to be the leader of the Arab cultural renaissance.

His quest was to revive and sustain Islamic and Arab culture and language while espousing a western mode of thought. He became an advocate of liberal thought and to this end translated many valuable works from and into Arabic. Before Taha Hussein, the Classical Arabic language was stagnant and heavily clichéd, and was presumed to be beyond the reach of the general populace. He breathed life into the language. His own style was quite easy for the general reader to comprehend, yet it adhered strictly to the principles of the language and fully employed its great richness of expression and vocabulary. He opposed dependence on the dialects of the various Arab nations, recognizing the need for a common language to sustain Arab unity. Otherwise, he argued, the Arab nations would suffer the same problems of isolation suffered in Europe due to the language barriers.

Taha Hussein strongly believed in the Egyptian revolution of 1952, in Arab unity, and in social reform. He fought fiercely for free education in Egypt, insisting that "knowledge is like water and air," the natural right of every human, and he made this his condition for accepting the post of Minister of Education in 1950. The new government subsequently declared free primary education, a policy that remains in effect to this day. Millions of Egyptians owe their literacy to Taha Hussein. His daughter, Amina, was among the first Egyptian women to graduate from university. She and her brother Moenis later translated his novel *Adib* ('The Intellectual') into French under the title *Une Aventure Occidentale*. This is a deeply sympathetic story describing the cultural shock suffered by an Egyptian friend during the years he spent in France.

Taha Hussein lived a life of constant struggles—political, social, and personal. His trilogy, *al-Ayam*, translated into many languages, recounts his life until he left for further study in France. After his death, his biography was completed by his son-in-law, Mohamed El Zayyat, in a book entitled *Ma ba'd al-ayam* ('Beyond the Days').

Taha Hussein's works can be divided into three categories: scientific study of Arabic literature and Islamic history; creative literary works with social content combating poverty and ignorance; and political articles. The latter he published in the two papers of which he was editor-in-chief after being expelled from his post as professor of Classical Arabic literature at the Egyptian University. His expulsion came as a result of public reaction to his book *On Pre-Islamic Poetry*, published in 1926, which gave full expression to his modern method of literary criticism.

His novels express an astounding sensitivity, insight, and compassion in that age for a person with his background. His arguments for justice and equality are supported by a deep and honest understanding of Islam. Equally remarkable are his empathy with his downtrodden compatriots and his understanding of women's deepest emotions and thoughts as girls, lovers, wives, and mothers.

The stories in this book were first published as articles in the periodical *al-Katib al-Masri* ('The Egyptian Writer') in 1946. When they were later compiled in book form in 1947, the government realized that their social content revealed many of its shortcomings. It banned the book and pressurized the periodical to stop publishing the articles. The book was finally published in Lebanon and only came to be published in Egypt after the 1952 revolution.

Taha Hussein, who had to bear the brunt of conservative attacks and confront many enemies of his reforms, enjoyed the affection of his pupils and colleagues. During his lifetime, he was elected a member of many educational academies in other Arab countries, and was honored by many international institutions. The American University in Cairo paid no heed to the Egyptian Prime Minister Isma'il Sidqi, when he warned anyone against offering employment to Taha Hussein. Its Ewart Memorial Hall, where it held its extra-curricular activities, was teeming in the 1930s with listeners eager to hear him and to declare him the new Dean of Arabic Literature.

He was awarded honorary doctorates from French, British, Spanish, and Italian universities. President Gamal 'Abd al-Nasir bestowed on him the highest Egyptian decoration, *Qiladit al-Gumhuriya*, normally reserved for heads of state. In 1973 he received the United Nations Human Rights Award.

Taha Hussein died in October 1973, immediately after witnessing his country's victory in its last war against Israel. He died in his home, alone with his 'sweet voice,' who later wrote in *Ma'ak*:

> We were together, alone, close to an extent beyond description. I was not crying—the tears came later.

No one knew of what had happened. Each of us was before the other. Unknown and united as we had been at the beginning of our journey. In this last unity, in the midst of this very close familiarity, I talked to him, kissing that forehead that was so noble and handsome, on which age and pain had not succeeded to carve any wrinkles, and no adversity had managed to cause to frown—a forehead that still emanated light.

For before anything, and after everything, and above all things, he was my best friend, and he was, with the import the word holds for me, my only friend.

Introduction

To these burning with their yearning for justice
And to those rendered sleepless by their fear of justice
To these and those together
Do I direct these words

To these who have what they do not spend
And to those who do not have anything to spend
Are these words directed.

I cannot find a more accurate means of depicting Egypt
during the later years of the monarchy than these two dedi-
cations. During those distant yet recent years, Egyptians
formed two groups. One represented the great majority of
the wretched, who burned with a yearning for justice in
wakefulness, in sleep, and in the darkest hours of night.
The other represented the small minority, which cowered
from justice when confronted by the light of day and was
terrified of it when engulfed by the dark of night.

He who belonged to the majority was unable to secure
the means of his livelihood and the livelihood of those
whom he supported. Thus he suffered his own deprivation
and underwent the greatest and most hateful anguish in
seeing the deprivation endured by his children.

His eye was capable of coveting objects at the farthest
reaches of sight, yet his hand had no reach at all. He
would see delicacies at arm's length, and his heart would

long for them and the hearts of his sons and daughters would long for them. Yet when he attempted to grasp them, his hands would refuse to stretch out, as though paralyzed or as though bound to his body by the heaviest of chains.

He would suppress his frustration and bid himself be patient with what he hated and bid his family be patient in the face of suffering and adversity, and he would await justice—but justice loitered and was very tardy in answering his call.

He saw many blights attacking his body and spirit, and the bodies and spirits of his children. He would resolve to remedy their damage, but his ordeal would confine him and weaken his determination and he would be obliged to surrender himself and his family to these blights to work their will.

He had resigned himself to ignorance, since his father had not been able to educate him. He strove to extract his children from the ignorance to which he had been confined, but could not find the means to do so. Thus he accepted ignorance for his children as he had accepted it for himself, and he awaited justice that would allow them some of the enlightenment he had been denied in his youth. But justice loitered too long and was very tardy in answering his call and his children's call.

He found wretchedness his detestable companion. It accompanied him when he set forth, and remained with him when he went home. It lived with him and his family in their home—if he and his family were allowed a home in which to find shelter.

He would bid himself be patient with that detestable companion and he would bid his family be patient, certain that he was incapable of escaping it since he could neither hide underground nor flee to heaven. He awaited justice, which would rid him and his family of this despised companion. But justice loitered and was very slow to answer his call.

Wretchedness would only accompany this majority along with its friends: hunger, nakedness, sickness, humiliation, degradation, toil that consumes and is never exhausted, and anxiety that intensifies and never relents. The people felt the greatest hatred for these companions and were most weary of them. But they found no means of ridding themselves of such burdensome wayfellows unless justice should come and drop a veil between them. But justice loitered and was excessively tardy in coming, as though walking in chains, hardly taking a few steps when some force would pull it back to its resting place, where it remained, as far as it could possibly be from those who loved it and whom it loved, who pined for it and for whom it yearned.

Thus did they aspire for justice, burning with ambition, yet did they attain nothing. Many are the generations that went by, obtaining of justice no more than a longing and consuming passion for it.

As for the second group, that of the smallest minority, its members witnessed the wretchedness of the majority, its misery and its suffering, its subjugation to affliction and misfortune, its submission to catastrophe and mishaps, but they cared not for what they saw, and paid no heed to it.

Perhaps they saw nothing and felt nothing, being too engrossed in their prosperity to notice the hardship of those around them. Their luxury distracted them from the distress of others. They were heavy with wealth and did not care that others were burdened by poverty.

Their sight was as short, yet their reach as long, as it was possible to be. They would desire, and were able to satisfy their desires until they were weary of them. They would want, and obtain, until they were bored of their wants. Their hearts had become as hard as rock, or even harder. For there are rocks from which rivers gush, there are rocks that crack to allow water to pass, and there are rocks that collapse in fear of God.

Their minds had been screened from what was around them, their surroundings had been veiled. For they could not see the warnings that filled the world they lived in.

If they noticed, they would turn aside and compound their stupidity and vanity. They neither thought of what was nor pondered what could be, but lived for the hour at hand as though every day had been severed from time, having neither a yesterday nor a tomorrow.

The gap between them and that suffering, wretched group grew wider. They would become aware of this group only when they needed it and if they needed it. They showed it no mercy or compassion, but would conde-scendingly command it to derive for them happiness from its misery, comfort from its drudgery and luxury from its destitution.

Governments, willingly or unwillingly, strove to please the prosperous. Perhaps some government members at-tempted to steal some reforms, looking upon the wretched of the earth with some compassion and endeavoring to touch them with a wing of mercy. But hardly would they start to do so, than they would find the earth quaking be-neath them and find themselves isolated and bombarded by lecture after lecture, commanding them to comprehend that the aim of government was to increase the prosperity of the affluent and intensify the destitution and suffering of the wretched.

These words were serialized during the latter years of the monarchy. The government then in power took no heed of them and paid them no attention. But one day they were assembled into a book so that they might reach the hands of all readers and counsel the spendthrift, enlighten the privileged, and console the deprived.

Then did the government take heed and pay attention to them, pausing briefly before them only long enough to is-sue the directive that this book should not reach the people and that its copies should be lifted from the press and dealt with as seen fit by the ruler. They should be burned or torn or drowned or be inflicted with whatever God willed from among the various trifling options before Him—as long as they did not reach the readers' hands.

Thus was this book confiscated, among others that were meant to enlighten Egyptians with the reality of their affairs, counseling the tyrants and oppressors, and consoling the wretched and desperate.

And Egypt beheld—Egypt, which thought it was the shelter of freedom in the Near East, the leader of the Arab peoples, leading them toward dignity and pride and independence, which thought it had protected the free men of Syria, Lebanon, and Iraq from the oppression and tyranny of the old Turkish Empire—that same Egypt beheld a book written by one of its sons being kept from its citizens and finding its way to Lebanon, where it was printed and published and distributed throughout all the Arab countries, before returning to Egypt and entering it with fear and caution, its readers literally hiding with it. When it was printed and published in Lebanon again, Egyptian readers heard of this and condemned it in their souls but could not proclaim their condemnation.

Thus Egypt had gone back to the times of France in the seventeenth century, when some of its writers would escape with their books to have them printed in Holland, fearing the might, violence, and oppression of the censor.

I try to comprehend the source of the fear that turned the government against this book, causing it to deprive it of life in Egypt, and I am unable to understand. There are no political arguments nor anything resembling politics in this book. It contains no unlawful instigations against the social system. It holds no enticements to what were then called 'destructive principles.'

Each of its chapters had already been published in a magazine or a current newspaper without being condemned by the government, nor did it displease the public prosecutor, nor was its author or its publisher taken to court.

Fear is therefore the pitfall of oppression, and it is panic that precipitates tyranny. The government bridles the au- thor as a means of bridling his book. It responds to whim and succumbs to passion. It rules the people according to love and hate, rather than on the basis of truth and justice.

I know of no persons more foolish, nor more ignorant, nor more stupid than those who rule by the dictates of fear and panic, of passion and whim, of love and hatred. For they entangle themselves in an endless array of absurdity. They think that everything is within their power although theirs is a limited human power with boundaries beyond which they cannot reach. They confiscate a book in Egypt and think that they have stood between it and the Egyptian people—only to find that it has been published in Lebanon and has returned to Egypt, where people have read it.

All that the government wove has been unwound, and all that it plotted has been undone. People scrambled for the book and competed to obtain it, whereas if the government had cleared the way, some would have read it, and some would have shunned it. They think they understand every- thing and that their minds extend to reaches that the minds of others cannot attain.

Yet their minds are human, capable of understanding lit- tle, unable to grasp plenty. Had their minds taken note of all the articles being published in the newspapers, and all the books being circulated by the presses, they would have impeded all the papers and closed down all the printing presses.

What greater evidence of this lack of understanding is there than that new form of literature which that tyrannical government created, where writers were obliged to turn away from candor to the arts of implication and insinua- tion, of allusion and typification?

This type of literature became an independent form, and the readers competed in it passionately, reading and interpreting, discussing their interpretations and analyses, and extracting clear meanings from ambiguous allusions.

Look at this author's publications: *Gannat al-shawk* ('Paradise of Thorns'), *Gannat al-hayawan* ('Paradise of Animals'), *Mir'at al-damir al-hadith* ('Mirror to Contemporary Conscience'), *Ahlam Shahrazad* ('Sheherazade's Dreams'). You will find allusions to phenomena that we abhorred and could not speak of openly during those dismal days. We preferred ambiguity to clarity, symbols and riddles to declaration, allusion and insinuation to calling things by their names.

The government of that era and its controllers would read and not understand, and would clear the way between the writers and their writings, and between the readers and this new literary form being circulated among them.

Thus did literature defeat the oppression of the tyrants and escape the censorship of the censors and manage to record the injustices of the unjust and the corruption of the corrupters. It founded a new language between itself and the readers, understood by both them and the writers, and a new art form appreciated by the readers, one that they liked and preferred to the forms of open declaration and clarity.

Literature is most similar to a great, strong river that gushes forth from its sources, carving its course until it reaches the sea, vanquishing the difficulties it encounters, breaking through whatever obstructions stand in its way, adopting whatever stratagems it requires to make its way to its destination. For the injustice of the unjust, the violence of the oppressors, the arbitrariness of the censors are all too weak to stand in the way of literature and art, or to come between them and the readers.

Oh, what dim, dark nights those were, densely overcast, when the stars were not allowed to send forth their shining arrows, when the moon was not allowed to spread its gentle, beautiful light, when layers of darkness pressed down and overlapped.

Almost suffocating, we bore their oppressiveness and sustained their heaviness, yet we nevertheless continued to send forth our hot, scorching breaths, like blazing torches illuminating the way for our readers and guiding them toward the means of realizing their aspirations.

And here now is the honest dawn, pointing at the overlapping, interlocking layers of darkness with those pink fingers mentioned by poets, defeating and dispersing them as though they had never crowded in or pressed down.

Only days and weeks have passed and behold, the faint dawn is spreading and expanding and drowning the world with light and beauty, with righteousness and justice.

Here the author has no need for devices to express his innermost self, nor a symbol by which to conceal the secret of his heart from the censors. Here he speaks to his readers with honesty and clarity, with ease and contentment.

He portrays to them a tranquil life, a comfortable subsistence and widespread justice after depicting the hell of destitution, oppression, and misery.

God has confirmed dreams and realized hopes and made of our successful revolution a support of righteousness, an upholder of justice, an implement of equity, and a course of equality.

For the sufferers of the earth, He has exchanged wretchedness with mercy, unhappiness with joy, and destitution with well-being.

Saleh

"When you hear the shaykh raising his voice with the last *Allahu akbar*, tell me. If you do that, then you are truly my son."

The boy smiled at his mother, who had been speaking to him while stroking his cheek, and said, "And if I don't, then whose son would I be?"

The boy's mother was taken aback for a moment, and her sons and daughters around her laughed. But she slapped the boy's cheek tenderly and said, "You have a cheeky tongue and are given to argument." Then, slipping a piece of sugar in his hand, she repeated, "When you hear the shaykh raising his voice with the last *Allahu akbar*, tell me, and if you do so, you will get another like it before you sleep."

The boy bit the sugar eagerly, saying, "Now that makes sense!" Then he darted out, followed by the laughter of his mother and of her sons and daughters around her.

The house was in a bustle that evening as guests of influence and importance in the province had arrived. They had not come empty-handed bringing with them many rare objects as presents.

The mistress of the house was always keen to be hospitable to guests and so was waiting for the last *Allahu akbar* with which the shaykh would raise his voice, ending his sunset prayers.

The various courses had been prepared and were waiting to be served as soon as the guests were done with their prayers. The *tharid*, the first of these courses, was almost ready. The bread had been cut into little pieces and placed in a large dish and the broth had been prepared, as well as the rice. The garlic had also been diced. However, the final touches to this dish should only be done at the last moment to avoid the bread becoming soggy with the broth, and to prevent the aroma of the garlic and the vinegar it has been browned in from escaping. The rice should also not be allowed to grow cold, or the melted ghee that has been poured over it will coagulate.

For all these reasons the boy had to listen to the prayers of the shaykh until he raised his voice with the last *Allahu akbar*, when he should rush to his mother and tell her, and she, in turn, would rush to these mixtures of bread, broth, garlic, vinegar, and rice and combine them in the large dish awaiting them. Once dinner had begun with this dish, it would be followed by the other dishes in their own time, for there is no harm in delay.

Yet the boy told his mother nothing, because he heard nothing. He was distracted from both the first and the last *Allahu akbar* by a serious matter. The shaykh and his guests finished their prayers. They sat down to talk and wait for the dinner that would be brought to them. The shaykh was restless as he waited. He was not accustomed to such slackness when entertaining guests. More than once he thought of clapping his hands to inform the household members that they were waiting. But he was embarrassed to do so, disliking the idea that he would be suspected of needing to warn the household and that it, in turn, would be suspected of inattention and carelessness. So he continued conversing with his guests in a raised voice. One of his daughters, passing behind the door, heard this loud conversation and rushed to her mother telling her what the son had neglected to tell her. An instant later the guests were at their table, eating noisily.

The boy had meant well. He had taken up his observation post in a nook of the courtyard where several pieces of iron, which he considered to be his treasure, lay. He would often sit alone there, gathering and separating the iron, and pounding the pieces against one another. This was the pastime in which he indulged, sometimes alone, sometimes with his little sister.

He sat in his little nook with his iron and he decided to play with it as soon as he had finished eating the sugar, while lending an ear to the shaykh and his guests, listening to their prayers and waiting for the moment when the shaykh's voice would rise with the last *Allahu akbar*. He would then hurriedly slip to his mother to tell her, before returning to his play.

But he had hardly settled down in his nook and started to gnaw on the sugar, when he felt a hand on his shoulder. He looked up and saw his classmate, Saleh, leaning toward him, touching his shoulder with one nand and holding in the other a bunch of wild flowers, which he offered with a smile.

He looked at Saleh and was horrified by his tattered clothes. His chest showed more than it should. His shirt was split at the shoulders, revealing them unbecomingly. His garment was threadbare and filthy—it bared more of the boy's body than it covered. It seemed to be a collection of tatters sewn together and hung on a weak and feeble body to conceal whatever they could, so that it would not be said that he was going naked.

The boy raised his head and saw Saleh's face, pale and full of misery, but with a smile full of sadness and hope.

He saw two restless eyes flitting around, down to the iron bars scattered on the ground, up to the piece of sugar in the boy's hand, and further up, toward the grape vines hanging on the wall and over the posts supporting them.

Saleh's hand was still extended to his companion with the artless, coarse bouquet of wild flowers. He said, "I didn't want to go home without coming and giving you these buds that haven't bloomed yet. Take them and put them in a container with some water and wait until morning. They will open up and become beautiful, sweet-smelling flowers!"

The boy said nothing. He took the flowers and gave Saleh what remained of the piece of sugar in his hand, beckoning him to sit down and join him in play.

Saleh took the sugar and contemplated it for a long time. He brought it close to his mouth, and took it away again. Then he gave it a last, short look and quickly stuffed it in his cheek and waited for it to melt slowly, prolonging his pleasure. Then he sat down and began to turn over the pieces of iron with his friend.

The silence between them did not last long. They began to talk about the *kuttab* (the school where they learned the Quran), their classmates, the field, and the villages. All this made the boy forget about the shaykh's prayers, the guests, and the news he should have taken to his mother. Only the voice of his sister calling him to dinner from behind the door startled him.

The shaykh and his friends had finished their dinner, as well as the last prayer and what invocations followed it. The night-time coffee had been served. The mistress of the house, assembling her sons and daughters to dinner, had noticed our naughty friend was missing and had sent his sister to search for him.

When the boy heard his sister calling him, he hesitated in answering her as he did not know how to deal with his friend. But Saleh's low, sad voice was saying, "Answer. You are being called to dinner."

The boy said to Saleh, "And have you had your dinner?"

Saleh answered, "I will have dinner when I go home," and he stood up heavily and turned to leave. Had he been able to, he would have stayed. But he went.

The boy went back to his mother, carrying the flowers. When she saw him she reprimanded him for forgetting her order. But she asked him who had brought him the flowers. With a quiver in his voice, the boy said, "Saleh, the son of Hajj 'Ali brought them to me."

"And you gave him nothing?" his mother asked.

"I gave him what I had left of the piece of sugar," said the boy.

His mother replied, "And what do you think he can do with the piece of sugar? Do you think he can ward off his hunger with it? Did you not ask him to stay for dinner?"

Confused, the boy said, "I started to, but didn't dare."

His mother said, "Follow him quickly and bring him back to have dinner with you."

The boy darted out like an arrow, barely passing through the door before calling his friend. He did not need to run any further, nor did he need to repeat his call. For Saleh was standing in front of the house, leaning against the wall, staring in front of him. He had one leg forward, the other backward, wanting to go, and wanting to stay. When he heard his friend calling him, he answered meekly, "Here I am, what do you want?"

"I want you to stay to dinner," said the boy.

Saleh said nothing but turned to his friend and quietly followed him, his head downcast, as a dog follows his master when summoned.

When the boy closed the door behind him he found that one of his sisters had placed a stool in his nook. On it was a round tray with all the dishes that had been offered the guests. She had chosen not to share the dinner with the family and had insisted on serving the two companions.

When they had finished eating, Saleh left with a full stomach, and the contented boy returned to his mother.

Stroking his head, she told him, "If a classmate of yours visits you at dinner time, you mustn't let him leave without inviting him to share your meal." Then, after a short pause, she said, "Do you know that Saleh only brought you these flowers to be invited to dinner?"

"I didn't know," answered the boy. His mother said, "He saw the guests when they came, and he saw the presents they brought, and realized there would be plenty to eat in the house this evening. He wanted to get some of it, and so used these flowers as a pretext to come to the house."

"If only you had seen his clothes and how his chest and his back and his shoulders showed through them!" exclaimed the boy.

His mother said, "When you come out of the *kuttab* tomorrow, persuade him to come with you. I have some of your clothes to give him."

Then she turned her attention to her other sons and daughters, talking to them about the guests and the dinner. She reprimanded one daughter for having forgotten to stir the rice when she dropped it into the boiling water, almost turning it into a sticky, useless dough. For rice should not coalesce, nor should its grains be allowed to stick together. Each grain should be separate. She praised the other daughter for being careful with the *faluzag*. She had not prepared it as a liquid that runs off the spoon as a soup would, nor had she made it so solid that it would need to be cut into pieces. She had not neglected to stir it, and so had avoided the disagreeable lumps that make it unpalatable and difficult to eat. It had been smooth and pleasant to the tongue. Hardly had it entered the mouth than it was summoned by the throat. It was also light and tasty.

While she was talking to her daughters about these things, by which she taught them the art of cooking, and while her listening sons laughed heartily, the boy interrupted her and asked her why Saleh had not had dinner at his home.

"Didn't I tell you that he knew we had lots of delicious food and that he wanted to get some of it?" asked his mother.

The boy said, "But I see guests calling at our neighbors and I know they will have many delicacies, yet I don't go to their children and try to get some of what they have."

"Because you don't need to, since you're not deprived," she said.

"So Saleh is deprived, then?"

His brothers and sisters were getting annoyed at his persistence, but his mother was amused, and said, "Because your father has a source of livelihood, while Saleh's father has been reduced to poverty."

"Why?" asked the boy.

"You are a chatterbox," answered his mother. Then she turned to the eldest of her daughters and said, "Take him to bed. It's late and time for him to sleep."

Next morning, the boy woke up and went to his *kuttab* as he did five days a week.

It might occur to the reader to ask me about this boy. What is his name? Where does he come from? Who is his family? Who may he be? If these questions have occurred to the reader, I would answer him—as Diderot used to answer his readers when he imagined they were questioning him about aspects of his novels—that he is taxing both himself and me with questions, the answers to which might be useful in rendering a novel symmetrical and well built, its parts in harmony and enjoying the proper sequence of events as required by the old critics. But I am not trying to construct a novel and thus do not have to make it obey the literary laws outlined by the great critics.

For a novel to be perfect, the place and time must be specified, and the identity must be revealed of the persons to whom events are happening or who cause these events and of those who are exposed to misfortunes or who contrive them.

I am not writing a novel that obeys artistic principles, and, had I been, I would not have taken it upon myself to submit it to these principles. For I do not believe in them, nor do I attend to them, nor do I admit that the critics— whoever they may be—are entitled to set down for me any rules or laws whatsoever. Nor do I accept from the reader, however high-placed he may be, any interference between me and whatever words I set forth. They are but words that occur to me and that I dictate, then publish. Whoever wishes to read them may do so and whoever grows weary of reading them may turn away. Whoever wishes to approve of them may do so with thanks, and whoever wishes to be scornful of them may also do so, with thanks.

The important thing is that words should occur to me and that I should dictate and publish them and that the reader should find that which allows him to practice his freedom of will, which is capable of either enticing him to read or impeding him from doing so.

It is also important that the reader should feel that he has a selective taste by which he can recognize art and by which he can accept or reject it; this is no small matter. I do not want the reader to think that I am lording over him, or that I am being unfair to him. For I am the last person to be domineering and the least likely to be unjust.

I have a most intense love and respect for the reader. But I do not like him to dominate me or to be unjust to me either. Nor do I want to force my taste on him, as I would not like him to force his on me. Freedom should be the sound basis for the relationship between the reader and myself, when I write and when he reads. If I respond to these questions and thus reveal the home town of this boy and his environment, and if I make known his family, then this narrative will be longer than I like.

There is not only one boy in this narrative, there are two: one of them is Saleh, who makes of the wild flowers a means of obtaining his dinner, and the other is that boy at whose home Saleh finds that dinner. To be fair, I admit that the reader might be entitled to my revealing the second boy's name, since I have named the first, thus making things easier for him and avoiding confusion of the boy whose name and whose father's name he knows with the other of whom he knows nothing.

Actually, when I started dictating this narrative, I had no name for the second boy, and I still do not. For the person of this boy, and of Saleh, did not interest me. Rather it was the events that occurred to both of them that concerned me.

It is most probable that this Saleh never existed, because he fills the kingdom of Egypt from east to west and from north to south. He exists in the villages and in the cities and in all places. He fills Egypt with prosperity and good, yet he causes people to feel that Egypt is a country of wretchedness and misery.

I hold that the reader of this narrative, whatever he may be, cannot spend one day of his lifetime, or one hour of his day, without seeing this Saleh who cannot find money to spend and who wishes only to be allowed the means to find lunch or dinner at the home of his classmate, for whom we have not found a name until now.

Let us then agree that his name is Amin and that he attends the *kuttab* along with a very few of his equals who live in relative ease, and very many of his peers who are overshadowed by that luxuriant, beautiful shadow, the shadow of wretchedness, misery, deprivation, and the seeking—from this or that friend—of what may sustain them.

Saleh never existed because he fills the kingdom of Egypt. If something is overabundant, then it does not exist, whether philosophy approves of this statement or not.

As for Amin, he exists without a doubt because we see him, and hardly see anyone else. He is of great importance. He is that boy who does not go to bed hungry when night falls, and who, in the morning, does not go hungry to the *kuttab*. He does not wait long for lunch when it is time for it. He does not wait long for dinner when dusk falls, because it is his right to have his meal at the right time, and to get his share of sleep so that his precious health is not exposed to harm.

This young boy, or this young man, whose name we have agreed is Amin, undoubtedly exists because he does not fill the villages or the towns. He is a privileged person whose contemporaries and equals can be counted exactly in every village and town. Therefore he exists, because his number is limited and because we can investigate, enumerate, and prove him.

Here the reader's head is raised and on his face there is an ironic smile. His eyes shine with the twinkle of victory as he asks me in an icy, charming voice: "You wanted to avoid length by not answering our questions; but aren't you now entrenched in prolongation with this lengthy, ineffective, and fruitless statement?"

Excuse me, dear and noble reader! On the contrary, these words carry great benefit. For you meet a thousand Salehs every day without attaching importance to any of them, nor even recognizing their existence. Many a time have you met them, and long has been your association with them, until living among them has become an easy, familiar affair, not worthy of your attention or thought. Living in the midst of wretchedness, misery, and deprivation has become as natural and as comfortable as living with health and vigor—until you take as little notice of this as you take of the air you breathe or the light by which you are guided.

You see one or two Amins once in a while. Each of them overwhelms your heart and your mind and excites your attention and your contemplation.

Which do you think is better? That I should draw your attention to that wretched, poor Saleh who has filled Egypt with prosperity and wealth and whose life Egypt has filled with misery and unhappiness? Or is it better that I talk to you of Amin and of his home town and family, so that this story may be consistent and well-balanced, so that it may be worthy and ingenious and adhere to the principles of art as outlined by the critics? I personally prefer to address myself to your heart and whatever emotions are moving therein, and to whatever feelings are breathing therein, than to address myself to your mind, your taste, and your critical nature and to respond to your curiosity.

I prefer to talk to your heart, and to turn your attention to that Saleh who exists, and exists in plenty, until we have come to believe—or almost come to believe—that he is nonexistent. And who knows? Perhaps when I turn your attention to Saleh I will be referring you to yourself.

Do not be furious or angry. For I do not want—nor should I want—to hurt you or to suggest that one day you made of the wild flowers a means of obtaining some food, as Saleh did.

Rather I want to say that within each of us many Egyptians there exists something of Saleh. Saleh is the picture of wretchedness, misery, and deprivation. How few are the Egyptians that do not portray wretchedness, misery, or deprivation!

Wretchedness is not limited to that state reached through poverty (and its consequential hunger that tears the belly) and through privation that shreds clothing, exposing chests, backs, and shoulders.

Wretchedness can relate not only to hunger or privation, but to states that may be worse than both, for they involve the soul and the heart. I know of many people whose hands are full of money and whose share of wealth is so great that they are weary of it. Yet, despite this, they experience wretchedness and sorrow—and what sorrow! And they make of the wild flowers—or of the flowers carefully picked by young girls in the cities—a means of obtaining something from those who are less wealthy.

However it may be, the boy whose name we have agreed is Amin, went in the early morning to his *kuttab* as he was used to doing every morning and met his classmates, sharing amusement and study, lessons and play with them. He started to memorize what verses of the Quran he was assigned in class, but soon turned away from it to play with his companions. He had forgotten Saleh's story, remembering only that he was to return home with him at the end of the day.

Later, however, he was to be reminded of Saleh with worry and fear, then with consternation and terror, and finally with much pain and sadness. For he heard our blind master asking his sighted monitor, "Did you check the stamps?"

"Yes," answered the monitor.

"And were they all still there?" asked the master.

"Yes, except for Saleh's, the Hajj's son. It has faded. This boy is greatly in need of discipline. He neither obeys orders nor heeds advice, and always leaves the *kuttab* in the afternoon to plunge in the water."

Here the readers may ask—and how numerous are their questions—as they asked Diderot before me, about those stamps and what they may be. I must answer them. For most of them belong to a generation that has not attended the *kuttab* and does not know the story of the stamps and the water, while a few others have been separated through time from the days of the *kuttab* and such mishaps as occurred in it.

This story of the stamps used to take place in the *kuttab* every year in the summer, when the scorching heat had set in.

The boys liked to cool themselves in the water of the river or the canal when they came out of the *kuttab* in the afternoon or if they went home for lunch. They would rush to cool themselves by diving into the water, where they would play, swim, and race.

Their families were afraid for them and asked the master to take whatever disciplinary measures he saw necessary to restrain them from this dangerous sport. The master took a round piece of wood and carved something on it—I do not know not what. At dawn the monitor would dip this piece of wood in a red substance and stamp the thighs of those boys whom he suspected of being fond of sporting in the river and canal. The disappearance of this stamp was proof that the boy had broken the rule and had approached the great sin. These imprints, therefore, were checked every day and renewed if time had effaced them, and the boy punished if they had faded from his thigh too soon.

I do not know if the reader is aware that the monitor in the *kuttab* was the personification of bribery and corruption, just as the master was the personification of naiveté and harshness. But the boys used certainly to indulge in that great sin of theirs without care. The moment they left the *kuttab* they would rush to the water and throw themselves into it. They would buy the monitor's connivance with whatever offerings they could bring him from their homes, sometimes stolen but usually what was meant for themselves.

Saleh had nothing for himself or for the monitor, and the monitor felt that Saleh had neglected giving him a bribe for too long. He never asked himself whether this shortcoming was due to inability or to deliberate cunning. He therefore wanted to punish him, and reported him to the master. Had he favored truth, he would not have singled out Saleh. Amin knew that very well, as did the other boys. For some reason, his heart suddenly filled with love, pity, and compassion for Saleh. As soon as he heard the sighted monitor denouncing Saleh to the blind master, he shouted at the top of his voice, "The monitor hasn't told you the whole truth. It is not Saleh alone who has lost his stamp but all the students, because they all go into the river or the canal, but they bribe the monitor with the presents they bring him. Saleh brings him nothing."

The natural consequence of this bravery was that the rod was turned on Saleh's feet, and the whip worked on them until they bled. Then the rod turned to Amin's feet and the whip touched his legs, but with gentle strokes that did not cause them to bleed. Amin nevertheless learned that honesty and bravery and telling the truth are traits that do not avail in all places. If the matter had stopped there, it would have been bearable.

But friends and classmates turned against Amin and Saleh, considering them their enemies. They started playing tricks on them, and teasing and harassing them.

Amin went home with Saleh, who could hardly walk on his feet, but found consolation and diversion in his friend. When Amin's mother saw the poor unfortunate boy she comiserated with him and gave him one of her son's tunics.

As soon as Saleh saw it his mind leapt with joy and he forgot both the rod that had bruised and the whip that had ripped his feet. He insisted on rushing to the water and washing himself. He would lose the new stamp, and would be open to the monitor's denouncement and the master's rage. But he could not wear this beautiful garment without washing away the traces of his old dilapidated, filthy rags.

Amin's mother said, "Don't worry. I will ask the master to spare you the rod and whip tomorrow."

The boy left. He was happy, cheerful, and gay. Amin said to his mother, "Won't you now tell me why the master beat Saleh so severely that his feet bled but only beat me gently?"

"Because Saleh lost the stamp by disobeying orders and swimming in the water. His mistake was serious, deserving a strict punishment. As for you, you went beyond the boundaries of seemliness when you said what you did about the monitor in front of your classmates. You deserved a more lenient punishment."

The boy said, "But even still, I only told the truth."

Laughing, his mother said, "Truth is not told in all places."

"How will I learn those places where lies should be told?" asked the boy.

"You will get to know all that when you grow older. Now go to your iron in that nook of yours and play with it and talk to it until you are called to dinner," said his mother, still laughing.

Amin went to his iron and played with it, talked to it, and made the noise and clamor God wanted him to make with it. But he soon turned away from his iron and his nook, went to his mother and asked her, "Why doesn't Saleh take presents and gifts to the monitor like the others do?"

"Because Saleh is deprived and poor and he cannot find anything to feed himself with, let alone to give to the monitor!" said his mother.

Amin said, "Why is Saleh poor and deprived and unable to find anything to feed himself with or anything to guard himself against the monitor's evil?"

His mother, annoyed by his persistence, said, "You've gone back to your chattering. Go see to your business and don't exhaust me."

But the boy did not go see to his business. He continued to pester his mother. She only managed to get rid of him when she showed him she was angry and threatened him until he was on the verge of tears. Then she felt sorry and put a coin in his hand, saying, "Go and buy a piece of candy with this."

The boy brightened up and answered, "I'll buy candy with half of it and give the other half to Saleh to give to the monitor tomorrow." Then he pranced away, raising his voice in song.

But Amin did not give the half piaster to Saleh, because Saleh did not go to the *kuttab* the next day. The boy first felt annoyance, then sadness, when he looked for his friend but could not find him. He waited for him until noon, and then realized that Saleh was not coming to the *kuttab* that day. But he soon forgot Saleh and his absence while playing with his friends. As soon as he was through with his lunch with the blind master and the sighted monitor, he went out on the pretext of attending the noon prayer. Instead, he bought such trivia as boys of his age do with the half piaster, and he played with his friends around the mosque. Then he went back with them to the *kuttab*. Neither the master nor the monitor suspected that he had not attended the prayer.

Saleh was absent from the *kuttab* day after day. Then one morning he appeared. He was depressed and sad and so weak he could hardly hold himself up straight. Amin looked and saw that he was in that dilapidated, filthy tunic again. He greeted his friend with a smile, attending to him and asking him about his long absence. Saleh tried to answer but his voice was trapped in his throat and heavy tears ran down his cheeks.

Amin was stunned, for he had never known of silent tears, nor had he known that boys could cry without the master's whip touching them. He did not know that they could cry without their fathers and mothers roughly reprimanding them with their hands or their words.

Saleh then revealed his story. It was a story that greatly saddened him and filled him with perplexity, doubt, and trepidation.

The tunic that his mother had given his friend had been a source of great misfortune and relentless harm to his wretched companion. He had gone out with his new tunic, happy and gay. His legs had almost raced ahead of the wind. His voice, raised in song, could have silenced the birds dancing in the mulberry branches.

He dived into the canal as did the best of his colleagues. He swam in the canal as did the most experienced. He raced them and beat them and came out happy, cheerful, and gay. His soul was full of contentment and his heart was full of joy. From his contented soul and happy heart there came a strange beauty that drew his friends' and companions' attention.

"We have never seen Saleh as we see him today: handsome and strong. He is bursting with liveliness and energy."

He put on his new tunic, his new-found pride verging on vanity. But modesty controlled him and held him in moderation. He was pleased with himself.

His friends' eyes were filled with a mixture of happiness and envy, of kindliness and resentment.

He went home at sunset, strutting along in his new clothes. He had folded his filthy old tunic and was carrying it under his arm, feeling abused and ugly in simply having to bear it. Could he have done so, he would have left it in the road. But he was too kind to do so, and too perceptive. He took his worn-out, filthy tunic to his father's wife. Perhaps she could make something out of it.

I do not doubt that the reader will pause here and ask himself, and would have asked me if he could: "Wouldn't it have been better to have informed us at the beginning of the story that Saleh had lost his mother and that he was living as an orphan, enjoying only whatever meager fatherly love he could secretly steal, that he daily suffered the hatred unleashed on him by the stepmother who had replaced his mother in the household?"

I do not doubt that the reader will add to this question an observation that carries some anger, sarcasm, and vexation. He will say to himself: "Had the writer obeyed in this narrative the rules and guidelines outlined for the novel by critics, he would have introduced Saleh to us at the beginning of his account. He would have told us of his mother's death and his father's remarriage. He would have spared us this needless surprise."

But I repeat what I said before. I am not composing a novel. I am narrating. And those who tell a story do not bother with introductions where they list the home town, the family, the time, the place, and such useless nonsense as is so greatly acclaimed by the experts.

Had I started this narrative with a clear and detailed outline of Saleh and Amin's characters, and of their relations, the reader would have been much annoyed with these lengthy introductions.

Some readers would have said: "Skip all this irrelevant talk and get to your point. We are not so stupid or absent-minded as to need all this preparation!"

And then again, who has told the reader that Saleh is an orphan and that his mother is dead? There is no doubt that Saleh was not an orphan, and that his mother was not dead, and indeed was more alive than people should be. That is, if it is true that life is measurable.

Whether the reader likes it or not, Saleh's mother was certainly alive, because I want it to be so. I do not care what others want. It is I who am creating Saleh from nothing or taking Saleh from the street.

For Saleh exists because he does not exist. He exists in reality because we see him in every house and every place.

He does not exist in reality because he fills the towns and cities and is burdening himself and the people by existing.

That which exceeds its limits turns against itself, as it is said. Therefore, I alone, as it is also said, know about Saleh what others do not know, and I decide that his mother did not leave the house because she died, but left the house because she was divorced.

I can do whatever I want with his mother after that divorce: I can make her stay divorced, working as a servant in other people's houses. I can find her a husband with whom to live happily and prosperously. I can reduce her to one of those occupations that wretched women like her live by.

Thus I could reduce her to selling vegetables. Or fruit. I could order her to bake bread in the homes of the rich and middle-class people. I could make her wash clothes in those houses. I could find her any occupation, because I am free to direct to the reader. Because the reader is obliged to receive my narrative as I direct it to him and he is then free to accept or refuse it, approve of it or scorn it.

In fact, I do not burden Saleh's mother with any of the occupations I have mentioned. I do not impose on her any of these plans because, in my freedom to do what I wish, I prefer to be faithful in the recounting of history.

History has told me that Khadija, Saleh's mother, had a bad disposition and was difficult to live with, and that Hajj 'Ali, Saleh's father, was not unjust or unfair when he divorced her one or two years after she had given birth to Saleh.

For this man was kind-hearted and had a pure soul. He loved nothing as much as he loved gentleness and calm. His wife Khadija, Saleh's mother, had an ugly, repulsive nature and was a hateful companion. She was garrulous and shouted often. Nothing pleased her and she approved of nothing.

The poor man was thus compelled to part from her. He kept his son Saleh in his care and tried to find the time to raise him, but could not. The accidents of life mean that those like him are obliged to work for a living. He could not work to earn his living and be free to bring up his child. He was also, after all, a man, who can only live as people do. He was therefore compelled to take to himself a woman to bring up Saleh and give him other children.

Khadija found herself another husband to help her in life and compensate for Saleh, who had been kept by his father after buying off the judge with a few kilos of milk. Can you blame me if life went on like this in the old days?

There is no better proof that Saleh's father was not to blame for leaving his wife than the fact that she also forced her second husband to divorce her after she had borne him a son, whom they had called Sa'id.

He left her for the same reasons that her first husband had left her. She was a bad companion, had a hateful disposition, talked too much and shouted too much. Nothing pleased her and she approved of nothing.

But as for her luck in this second divorce, I do not know if it was good or bad. How often it is that peoples' affairs

confuse the intelligent until they cannot differentiate between good and evil. What then can be expected of me,
who has had little luck with intelligence and who cannot
distinguish between happiness and sorrow?

One thing is certain, and that is that no sooner did
Khadija get divorced than the husband died, leaving her
Sa'id to bring up as she wanted, or as she could. But she
did not bring him up as she wished or could. Instead nature brought him up as it liked.

Many husbands discarded this woman, who was a bad
companion and who had a hateful disposition. Life became
burdensome for her, since she had little means and a dull
mind. So she started selling radishes and lupines. Then it
became so bad for her that she lost her mind.

Her madness was a gentle, calm one. Hearts were filled
with compassion for her yet people were afraid of her.
Thus she was named Khadija the Demoned.

She lived on the charity of the benevolent, while her son
grew in the shadow of this calm, frightful madness.

Her other son, Saleh, was growing in the shadow of his
stepmother, who at first showed him love and kindness,
then bore sons and daughters of her own and turned to
showing him hatred and antagonism.

Thus one of the brothers was brought up under sane hatred while the other was brought up under insane love.

Tell me, my dear reader, if it would have been better for
me to have set before you all these details at the beginning
of my narrative, until you had grown bored with Saleh and
Amin and of the anguish that all these words would have
brought to you? Or is it better that I should proceed by the
easy path I have chosen and tell you everything when it is
time to do so?

I know that you will be stubborn and will carry your
stubbornness and contrariness to all directions. Do as you
like. As for me, I have gone the way I have chosen and
have talked to you of the matter in the manner I have chosen.

*

I stopped a while ago, saying that Saleh bathed in the canal, put on his new tunic, and returned to his father's wife, happy with his new clothes, and offering his old ones that he carried under his arm.

But his father's wife looked at him from head to foot and liked his new tunic. She looked around the room and saw her own son and daughter. She saw they had two filthy tunics on like Saleh's old one, baring their shoulders as well as their backs and chests. She looked back at Saleh and his new clothing, then again at her two children in their old garments. Then she looked inside herself. A clear plan had been formed.

It was a hateful plan. The new clothing was not to be for Saleh but for her son Mahmud.

Hardly had dawn risen the next day than Saleh was met with his father's and stepmother's wrath. He was severely beaten and became sick for days. He was stripped of his new, beautiful garment and returned to his old, threadbare, filthy one. He had been unable to go to the *kuttab* the next day and stayed at home, prostrated in a corner, where he was cruelly neglected and terribly sick.

When he was able to walk, he went to the *kuttab*, only to suffer there from the monitor's hatred and the master's cruelty, but also to enjoy Amin's companionship.

Thus did Amin get to know the story of his wretched companion. His young mind did not know how to judge it. Had he not talked to his mother of Saleh's dilapidated, torn tunic she would not have given him the new one. Saleh would have continued his life of quiet and familiar wretchedness. He had wanted to do good for his friend but had caused him harm. Should he blame himself for that, or should he look for excuses? The truth is that he neither blamed nor consoled himself. Rather he turned to his friend to console and comfort him. He told himself that his kind, compassionate mother might find another tunic to dress his poor friend in.

But the reader is wrong, very wrong, if he thinks that life always proceeds in a familiar, logical manner, and that it always follows the thoughts and calculations people are used to formulating.

Life revolts no less against set conventions, drawn-up laws, and prepared plans than I do. Rather it proceeds as it wishes, not as people wish.

Saleh and Amin left the *kuttab* that evening. They reached the railway tracks that extend from north to south and from south to north. There they noticed a crowd of people shouting and calling each other. When they reached the crowd they beheld a sight that horrified and dismayed them. A body had been sliced in two and a thick sheet thrown over it to hide its unsightliness. They also saw a woman slapping her face, beating her breast, shedding her tears, and filling the air with coarse laughter.

The body was Sa'id's—'devoured' by the train, as was said in those days.

The woman was Khadija, whose instinct drove her to heart-break but whose madness drove her to laughter.

As for Saleh, he looked at his brother, and he looked at his mother and wanted to stop but preferred to go on with his companion as though he had seen nothing.

I do not know what the two friends did. I know only that Amin's father went to his family that night saying, "Today the trains have been greedy. One devoured Sa'id at noon, and the other devoured Saleh at night. Khadija the Demoned lost her two sons in one day." Then he turned and saw Amin, horrified, almost choking with tears. He patted his head and kissed his eyes and told him in a kindly voice, "You won't be going to the *kuttab* tomorrow morning because you're going to attend primary school in the provincial capital."

When Amin was older and had become a man of some importance he said, "I can still see the body and the thick cloth that had been thrown on it. Yet I look at the face and

I see not Sa'id's but Saleh's, though I did not see Saleh when the train devoured him."

Qasim

He walked in the deep darkness of night. Everything around him was calm. The world was enveloped in a dreadful, oppressive quiet. Had he raised his head to the sky, he would have seen scattered traces of faint light. But he did not raise his head to the sky, nor did he bow it toward the ground. Rather he went on, his gaze fixed straight ahead as though he were trying to penetrate the thick screen of darkness with his eyes. He turned neither right nor left, like some inanimate object merely carved in the image of a man. Had he run or hurried, he would have appeared like a flying arrow breaking through the dense layers of darkness before him. But he did not quicken his steps, proceeding calmly and confidently.

He pushed on as though urged forward by an invisible, gentle force. He moved placidly, taking his time. He hurried for nothing and stopped at nothing, but headed for his destination as time proceeds to its end: carefully, slowly, and with deliberation.

Had he been a poet or a reciter of poetry, or had he enjoyed some culture, he would have recalled those flowery fingers that motion to the dark of night, ordering it to subside. Or he would have imagined a tiny, pure silver arrow, cutting through the thick layers of darkness, defeating and destroying them. On the western horizon the stars fell as though some of them were inviting the others to escape.

He saw the light of dawn extending its delicate tongue from behind the river, and in the air he heard a weak, faint sound coming from behind and moving ahead of him toward the east as though greeting and welcoming the faint light.

Then he saw the light extending and stretching, until he felt the whole atmosphere vibrating with light and song.

The light woke the stones and told them of the rise of dawn, and the sound woke the living, and advised them that prayer was better than sleep.

All this reminded him of neither prose nor poetry, nor did it recall ancient or contemporary literature from the depths of his memory. For all this was nothing to him, nor was he aware of the existence of such things, or that they might even occur to people.

He was conscious only of what his brother, the blind shaykh, had told him one day: "You walk in the darkness of night and go far, and the road stretches ahead of you, frightful and unsafe. Memorize this verse from the Quran and repeat it in your heart or with your tongue, for it will dissipate your fear, and keep you company in your desolation."

Then he recited the holy verse:

> Who have believed and whose hearts have rest in
> the remembrance of Allah. Verily in the remem-
> brance of Allah do hearts find rest. (*XIII, 28*)

And so he never left his humble, tiny house to go to the river in the dark of night without this verse being continuously repeated in his heart, filling his soul with reassurance and tranquillity. If he felt a threat, near or far, the verse traveled from his heart to his tongue, his voice thrusting it out into space. He would then feel safe from every treachery and protected from every evil.

That night he walked ahead, the verse keeping his heart company, so that whatever he saw and whatever he heard, he was afraid of nothing and recalled nothing, but only stopped reciting and quickly asked himself if he should

proceed to the river before him or return to the mosque behind him where, having performed his prayers, he would
then go again to the river, to seek therein whatever fortune
God sent him.

He did not hesitate for long but returned to the mosque,
where he performed his prayers, speaking to no one and
being addressed by no one. Then he resumed his journey
to the river, calm, reassured, and alone. He remembered
nothing and barely thought of anything. He was a solid
object carved in the image of man, moving ahead deliberately and slowly, looking neither at the sky nor at the
ground, turning neither right nor left, unconscious of the
splendor of the defeated night and the beauty of the victorious morning. He was an inanimate object that had left a
decrepit home and proceeded to a wondrous river, seeking
whatever livelihood God sent it.

For Qasim was neither a poet nor an admirer of poetry.
He was not a lover of the splendorous night and the
beautiful morning. It did not even occur to him that the
night was splendid or that there was a beauty to the
morning.

For Qasim was only an ignorant, wretched, sickly man,
who sought from the river that which would help him to
bear his burden, and feed his wife Amuna and his
daughter Sekina in his squalid house.

Had it not been for the fact that Qasim used to repeat the
prayer in his heart, and to perform the dawn prayer if it
caught up with him on his way to the river, had it not been
for the fact that he engaged in the most elementary and
simple thoughts about selling whatever fish came out of
the river to feed himself and his family, had it not been for
all this his movement between his house and the river
would have been something completely instinctive, like the
movements of the ants and the bees in search of their
livelihood.

Qasim was sickly, exhausted by ailments, his body almost consumptive. He could not endeavor or strain or pul-

sate in the affairs of life as others do, but exerted a minimal effort to hold on to life for himself and for his small family. He would go to the river from time to time, and if God sent fish into his net he would sell them without exertion or barter, then return with whatever money this yielded him. With much listlessness and tedium he would buy whatever would alleviate his and his wife's and his daughter's condition. He would take these things home, thrust them into Amuna's hands, then, dejected and exhausted, move to a threadbare mat spread in a corner. There he would lie down, feeble and emaciated, remaining there, uttering no words and thinking no thoughts, until his wife had prepared whatever food she could and placed it in his hands. The three of them would then eat what they could.

Many were the nights when Qasim failed to rise and go fishing. Crushed by illness, he would remain fixed in his place, immobile and dumb, secreting in his soul regret and pain, if he were capable of experiencing regret and pain. Perhaps he would take upon himself more than he could bear and task his body beyond its endurance, and rise when unable to rise, and walk when unable to walk, and reach the river to find it generous to others and frugal to him, then go home, weary, saddened and empty-handed. He would cast a sad, sickly look at his wife and go to his mat to lie down, uttering no words and thinking no thoughts.

At these times Amuna would sluggishly go out to this or that house and help its members with some of their chores, returning at midday, carrying enough to hold on to life for herself and for her husband and daughter, and to ward off hunger.

That morning Qasim left the mosque after performing his prayers and walked to the river, confident in his heart and calm in his soul. On his lips, there appeared a faint, pale smile attempting to portray rest and contentment, but succeeding only in reflecting a quiet sadness carrying some slight hope.

The river happened to be generous on that day and God granted him some good fortune. His net came up with a huge fish. Hardly had he felt its weight and seen its size than his heart stirred with a faint joy, broadening the smile that had been drawn on his lips, and erasing the pallidness that had shaded it. A pale, faint light shone in his small eyes. He felt he would not be able to carry his catch very far, so he stood there looking at it, then at the river, then around him, raising his head to the heavens with thanks, and waiting for some healthy youth from the village to pass by and carry this catch for him to the house of the village headman.

For he had decided, as soon as he had seen this won-drous, beautiful catch, that it should not be sold in the market, but must be carried to the home of the headman—a wealthy man who showed him kindness and compassion, and who from time to time would ask him to bring to his home whatever good catches came his way.

One of the girls from the headman's household had risen with the morning before the family awoke from its sleep, and started to do as she was accustomed to do every morning of every day. She began sweeping the courtyard and restoring it to order. She arranged the chairs in their places and dusted the long bench that extended along the front of the courtyard, preparing it for the blind shaykh to sit on at sunrise, recite a verse from the Quran, drink his coffee, and engage in a sometimes lengthy and sometimes brief conversation with her, according to whether he was in a hurry or not.

While the girl was thus occupied, there was a light knock on the door. She opened it to find sad Qasim, with a faint trace of contentment and hope on his pale face, and a youth behind him carrying his burden.

Qasim and the youth greeted her. Then the two men came in quietly and put this great catch of theirs on the bench at the front of the courtyard. Qasim said in his low, sickly voice, "I have no doubt that the mistress will be pleased with this catch."

His companion started to leave, but the girl thrust something in his hand that he readily accepted before hurrying happily away. Qasim also started to leave, but the girl motioned him to stay.

She left him briefly and came back with some food and a cup of coffee. He ate and drank and blessed God.

While he was thus occupied, the blind shaykh came, as he was used to coming every morning, deliberately being forceful in pushing the door before him and raising his voice in an invocation of God, the veiler of unsightliness, meaning thus to alert the family to his arrival. He closed the door roughly behind him and moved to his bench at the front of the courtyard.

But hardly had he sat down than he leapt up in alarm and dread, possessed of a fear as blind as himself and which was at a loss as to how to manifest itself or in which of his members to appear. His face quivered, his body trembled, his hand moved to and fro in the air, his mouth gaped— revealing ruined teeth—and his voice vibrated with a rattle rising from his belly to his lips.

Qasim looks, and the girl looks with him, and they observe his panic, and they break out in loud, continuous laughter. The shaykh comes back to his senses, his fears put to rest, having thought that the boys and girls of the house had been plotting against him. He realized that no one had played a trick on him, and that Qasim had only made a mistake by putting the fish where it did not belong, and that the girl had been too preoccupied by the fish and the fisherman to think of the shaykh's coming, and so forgetting to prepare his seat. The blind shaykh laughed at himself, at Qasim, and at the girl, then sat on a chair and refused to recite the verse until he had drunk his pre-recital coffee. He also drank the coffee he was used to drinking after finishing his chanting, but as he got up to leave, he said, "God's wisdom is far-reaching. You have laughed at me and made me laugh at myself. But God wished me well. For I will not bear the expense of food for my family today. Tell the mistress, my girl, that this fish has filled my heart with terror, and that I am waiting for my share later in the day. I have do doubt you will make various dishes with it, so it will not be enough to send me only one dish—I must get some of each."

The blind shaykh left, content with himself, looking forward to this day in which God had made good fortune available to him without his pursuing it. For God provides for whom he wishes without accounting for Himself.

The whole family had been awoken by the blind shaykh's panic, by the fisherman's and the girl's laughter, and by the verses of the Quran.

They started to receive the morning as they were used to: some of them worked and some of them lazed about.

The fisherman remained in his place. Perhaps he had forgotten himself, or was waiting for the price of his catch, or perhaps he was pleased with the house where he had eaten and drunk, and by the consolation he found there from his affliction and ailment.

Whatever the case, the man of the house finally met him, addressed him kindly, and put some piasters in his hand. The fisherman left satisfied and happy. But he did not go home. Instead he turned and went to the market.

The reader will notice that we have reached a crossroads in this narrative. I can go to the market where Qasim the fisherman has gone, or I can go to the homes where the shaykh goes each morning to recite the Quran, drink coffee, and draw the members of the household into sundry conversations, his voice never weakening and his stomach never tiring from the cups of bitter coffee thrown into it. Then I could go to the *kuttab* where the shaykh will end up at dusk when the sun is on the verge of setting.

I could leave Qasim to buy whatever he wants at the market, and leave the shaykh circulating among the houses before ending up at the *kuttab*, and instead stay in the house, not leaving it, and following the fish where it has been moved from the courtyard and has settled in its place in the kitchen, between the oven and the long row of pots that vary in width and depth. I could watch the women approaching that great fish and cleaning it and cutting it and preparing it for the assortment of food they wish to make.

I shall not remain in the house, however, nor follow Qasim, nor follow the shaykh, but go out of the house and turn left and walk a while, then turn left again and walk some more, then right and a few steps forward. At the farthest end of a wretched narrow street I will find a humble room made of mud—not of stones, or of red bricks, or of sun-dried bricks, but of mud.

Chunks of this mud had been made into roughly equal blocks and mixed with chaff and chopped straw, then arranged next to each other until they rose some height in the air, enclosing a small piece of land. Palm branches were then cast across it to become the roof and a narrow, short board of thin wood was placed at the opening to become the door.

This is the house I prefer to the market and such goods as are exhibited there, and to the trade that takes place in it. I prefer it to the shaykh's houses and to whatever conversations they may contain. I prefer it to the *kuttab*, and to the work and play, the artlessness and cunning that may be found there.

I select that humble house because I would like to find Amuna and her daughter Sekina there. They have received the morning wretchedly as they had received the night miserably. They had been aware of Qasim getting up, heavy, dragging his legs. Closing the tiny door behind him, he had gently and carefully plunged into the heart of night, hoping to reach the river and to find his and their fortune therein.

They had felt him rising in the hollow of the night and they had not risen with him, and they had said nothing. And why should they get up? What was there for them to do? And why should they speak? What was there for them to say?

Qasim left and they stayed. The night contained them, motionless and asleep, as it contained him, awake and moving. The morning hung over them, silent and lingering, as it shone for him, pursuing his fortune.

They arose from their sleep when the sun arose, each of them sitting in her place, brooding, not knowing what to do, nor knowing what to say. They stayed there waiting for Qasim. Perhaps he would bring some fortune back with him.

It was their habit, if their waiting was prolonged, to have some dry bread to keep hunger away. Or perhaps they would leave the house to talk to their neighbors.

Sekina is a girl of seventeen. She is gentle and docile. She has a simplicity that resembles imbecility. There is a touch of beauty in her face that would have appealed to observers, were it not for the air of misery she projected. There is a symmetry to her body and proportion to her shape that are visible yet do not invite an urge to solicit her. For the girl is naked, or almost naked. Only tatters cover her body, revealing here and there a painful beauty.

Their gloom that morning did not last for long. Amuna suddenly asked her daughter in a listless, dispirited voice, "Didn't you get up and leave the house a short while after your father had gone out to the river?"

The girl answered, "Yes, I got up and left the house, but I came back in a second."

Amuna said, "I thought so, and expected you to come back in a second, but that second lingered and lasted for such a long time that I worried you had been harmed. I started to go out to look for you but forced myself to stay for fear that the neighbors might notice. I waited and waited until it was morning. Then you came back

stealthily, coming in slyly, and slipped onto your mat, being as careful that I should not feel your return as you had
been that I should not notice your creeping out of the
house. Where did you go? What were you doing?"

Sekina heard her mother's words with her head raised at
first, but very soon her head sank as though her muscles
and nerves, failing to hold it up, had let it drop. The girl
remained silent and still. Her mother repeated the question
time after time but obtained no reply. Amuna finally lost
her temper. Her serious expression changed into one of
hateful and violent anger.

In a choking voice she asked her daughter, "Will you tell
me where you went and what you were doing?!"

Then she turned to the right and picked up a dry stick
made from a palm branch that she used in turning and
baking bread. She turned to the girl, waving the stick and
saying in a choking voice, "Will you tell me where you
were and what you were doing?"

The girl said nothing, and the stick started to strike her
shoulders with such intense violence that she leapt up as
though sprung from the ground or as if something in the
roof had wrenched her upright. But she did not stand for
long, as the stick started angrily striking her body at ran-
dom.

The girl kneels down, her hands covering her face,
twisting in pain, driving back a scream that wants to escape and with which her throat almost explodes. Then
blind anger takes hold of Amuna: she is no longer a
woman but a furious demon. She lets go of the stick and
jumps up swiftly and lightly, knocking the girl onto her
face.

She grabs the wretched creature's hair in her hands and
pulls her mercilessly by it, kicking her all the time in the
face. The girl's voice explodes in a horrible scream.

Amuna throws herself over her daughter and presses her
hands to her mouth, warning her, in her still choking
voice, that it will be death if she does not restrain her

screams, compose herself, and tell her honestly where she had gone and what she had done when she had slipped out of the house in the dark of night.

The girl is suffocating from the weight of her mother's body and the constant pressure on her mouth. She is almost certain that she is about to die. But she struggles violently until she escapes her mother's weight and sits up.

A stubborn resolution appears on her face. She pushes her mother's hands away from her mouth, and says in a voice choking like her mother's, but also revealing defiance and obstinacy, "You want to know where I went and what I was doing when I slipped out of the house in the dark of night? Very well then. I met my aunt's husband not far from his farm and stayed with him all the time, then came back when the day was breaking. Now do you know what you were ignorant of? Are you pleased with what you've learned?"

Amuna was appalled, then she exclaimed in bewilderment, "Since when do young girls meet their aunt's husbands in the fringes of night? You meet him whenever you want in broad daylight!"

"I meet him in broad daylight and I meet him in the dark of night. That is his and my business. What's it to you? It doesn't concern you in the least," said the girl.

Here the stick resumed its thrashing of the girl's body, but she said to her mother in a voice she found hard to restrain, "You will take your hands off me or I'll shout to the neighbors for help."

The stick fell from Amuna's hand and she said, "The neighbors! Oh, scandal! Oh, shame!"

Then she bent double and started moaning, almost inaudibly.

The girl stayed where she was, brooding, in a trance, as though she were a piece of marble, but as soon as she allowed her eyelids to flutter, heavy tears flowed down her face.

*

The reader has a curiosity of which the least that can be said is that it annoys the writer and blocks his stream of thought, forcing him to stop when he would have chosen to go on with his writing, or compelling him to digress when he would have preferred not to go beyond the subject he is presenting.

The reader is not satisfied with my telling him that the girl's mother feigned unawareness, that the girl took advantage of her father's absence and slipped out of the house in the dark of night, and that she finally confessed to her mother—after the torture she had suffered—that she had gone out for sinful reasons, and that a loathsome sin existed between her and her aunt's husband.

The reader does not find this sufficient. He wants to know how this repulsive relationship developed between a young girl of seventeen and a man who had passed his youth and who was her aunt's husband. Were it not for the fact that I am kind to the reader and do not like to be hard on him or send him off disappointed in his inquiry, or rebuff or fail him when he wants to learn more, I would have gone on with my narrative as I had started it, and refused to deviate to the origin of this loathsome relationship. For talk of it is detestable.

But there is no escaping the unavoidable. It is the writer's prerogative to follow whatever path he desires in his writing, but it is also the reader's privilege to expect to understand clearly and plainly the books, articles or chapters presented to him by the writer.

The reader knows that Qasim had a brother who was a blind shaykh, and who had read him a holy verse from the Quran that would allay his fear and lessen his desolation. Now the reader must know that Qasim had an attractive, playful sister who had captivated the minds of many youths when she had been lucky, and when the world had smiled on her and when matters had gone smoothly for her. Then the world turned its back on her, as it does on many people. Her body began to wither and her beauty began to fade when she approached maturity and was within sight of old age. She might have been reduced to a wretchedness like that of her brother the fisherman, or her blind brother, had she not met Hajj Mahmud.

He was a man who lived on the outskirts of the town and who still enjoyed a residue of strength and youth. He also owned some acres of land, which he used for planting cereals.

The days had toyed with Hajj Mahmud as they had done with the woman. Then he felt a need for righteousness, so he assumed some composure, and undertook to maintain his piety, and became keen on performing his prayers. Then he went on pilgrimage, and came back dressed in the garb of veneration and with an air of purity. He took this woman as his wife and settled down to a tranquil life in which no one could see any harm.

And yet as though his instincts were stronger than his will, as though his inclination toward playfulness were greater than his aspirations to piety, as though his wife's approaching old age had replaced satisfaction and contentment in his soul with brazenness and greed, he would walk through the city with a distracted eye, gazing left and right and examining this object here and that object there, as though every variation in his expression and in the restlessness of his gaze indicated that in his soul dwelt an inclination toward evil and a propensity for the despicable.

He had been unkind to his wife's brother, eyeing him with contempt and speaking of him with disdain. He failed to give him a helping hand or show any compassion for his overwhelming poverty, wretchedness, and illness.

But he saw this man's daughter as a full and rounded girl, facing life with strength and beauty, though with wretchedness and misery as well. He did not soften to her wretchedness or feel compassion for her misery, but lusted for her beauty and coveted her attractions and sought the means to possess her. And how plenty are the means of seducing those smothered by deprivation.

One day he noticed this beautiful, wretched girl casting a look of great longing at one of those men who used to cir-culate in cities and villages carrying such trivial trinkets as aroused craving in the hearts of the destitute. They carry a gum that is chewed in the mouth and which the village people call *leban* while the prosperous townspeople call it *ladin*. And they carry another bag laden with various kinds of beads and a variety of cheap metal rings and bracelets.

The village women garland themselves with these ab-surdities. They make necklaces from the beads and deck their hands and elbows with the rings and bracelets. They adorn themselves by chewing the gum, which they turn in their mouths, intermittently producing a sound that entices full-grown men and growing youths.

Hajj Mahmud saw the wretched girl with her great beauty, yearning for some of the trinkets displayed by a peddler who was surrounded by women and girls of the city, taking his cheap trinkets and paying with their scarce money.

Sekina looks and yearns, but cannot take anything be-cause she cannot pay anything.

Hajj Mahmud feels for the girl, or rather his heart is bent toward her. He buys some of the trash, paying a meager sum and flooding the girl's heart with joy, drowning her spirit in ecstasy, covering her face with a gaiety that adds beauty to her beauty and splendor to her splendor.

From that day Hajj Mahmud's heart was filled with a sinful love for this simple girl. And from that day Hajj Mahmud started, from time to time, to visit the wretched family, always bearing some presents with him. He started with gentle talk and moved on to effortless help. He sin-gled the girl out with a sympathy that would have been uninterrupted were he not careful and cautious, and fearful of exposure.

Qasim and his wife received this new amiability, but wa-vered between the pleasure its advantages incurred for them and the slight misgivings it stirred within them. But need was stronger than precaution.

What is certain is that the girl developed confidence in this man and began to trust him. She grew attached to the modest presents he offered her from time to time. So she frequented her aunt's house more often, and an affection developed between her and this man whom she called her uncle.

Here, I think, the reader does not need me to carry him to the end of this disgusting narrative. He can reach it alone. I think he has waited long enough for Qasim, who had gone to the market with the headman's piasters in his hand or in his pocket. Let the reader look at him, if he so wishes, returning from the market: his hands are now laden with goods, and on his pallid face is a cheerless joy. He approaches his humble house slowly, with a heavy step, his heart filled with modest content. For he is going to feed his wife and daughter with things they are not accustomed to receiving from him except on the rare occasions when the river is generous or when the prosperous give them alms.

However deeply people are reduced to poverty, however encumbered by misery, however harmed by distress, there remains in their nature a streak of dignity that invites them to find, when they eat what they have earned by their own endeavor, a sweetness that is lacking when they eat what is given them without their having earned or striven for it.

Qasim is now experiencing some of this pride. He wants always to depend on himself, were it not that he is too wretched and feeble and subdued by illness to achieve such independence.

Anyhow, he walked slowly, with a heavy step. It did him no harm that the neighbors should notice him as he neared his house, and that they should see the goods he carried from the market, and say to themselves: "Qasim had good fishing today. He and his wife and daughter will be blessed with tasty food."

Some of them would say this with much kindliness and compassion, some with much envy and vexation. Qasim recognizes all this in their glances and expressions. He is gratified by the kindliness of the kind and the envy of the envious.

He reaches his home and pushes the thin, weak door and steps forward. His face is flushed, his eyes are twinkling and his lips are parted. His faint voice is about to bid his family good morning, his weary hands about to thrust the food they have borne into his wife's hands, and he is about to sadly laugh with her. But he steps in and stares.

He sees a woman shedding heavy tears, quiet and still. And he sees a weeping girl trying to stifle a sob.

Qasim is dumbfounded at first. Then he questions them. Then he repeats his question. And now his wife answers him, in a choked and faltering voice, with words that sear his heart like red-hot coals. And now his arms go limp, and now the delicacies he carried with so much joy and attention fall clattering to the ground. And now his eyes dim, his lips meet, then pucker. He moves to his tattered mat and wearily sits on it, then lays down, exhausted by the stress that has beset his thin body and sickly, weak heart. His wife hears a feeble voice, coming from far away, saying, "Had God given us a boy in her place, we would not have been exposed to this shame."

Then it repeats: "This shame."

Then the voice is silent for a while. It comes back fainter and more distant, saying, "Poor people should not give birth to girls."

Then the voice breaks off and his wife does not hear it again for the rest of the day.

He is neither asleep nor awake, but somewhere in between.

As the day advances she starts to eye the food, thinking of preparing it, but she turns away from it, remaining in her place, subdued and lifeless, her tears falling heavily when her eyes release them, ending when her eyes dry out.

The girl lies prostrate in her place. She is neither alive nor dead. Now and again she is seized by a shiver, then she is enveloped in torpidity and lifelessness.

That day the neighbors did not see Amuna coming out in search of wood. They did not see smoke coming from the house. That day the neighbors did not smell the aroma of food being cooked on the fire. They had anticipated all this when they had seen Qasim coming home with his hands full of goods.

The sun reluctantly went to its exile, and the dark of night advanced and suspended its black clothing over everything. It perched heavily and tediously over the village, compelling the people to go to their beds, and imposing calm and quiet over everything.

A faint light sprinkled the sky. From Qasim's bed a frail person, almost a ghost, arose. He slipped out of the house. He turned to no one and no one turned to him. He plunged into the dark of night, trudging slowly, although he would have liked to hasten; heavily, although he was weightless from within. He moved ahead, not raising his head to the sky, nor turning right or left. For the dark of night had infiltrated his soul, and his mind had become a black coal devoid of peace. The still of night had penetrated his heart and no echo resounded in his breast. He did not recall the Holy Verse.

> Who have believed and whose hearts have rest in
> the remembrance of Allah. Verily in the
> remembrance of Allah do hearts find rest.

Yet he felt no fear, for the whole of him had been transformed into fear.

He bypassed the mosque on his way to the river. Before him the faint light of dawn approached from the east, faint, stretching upward and outward. Behind him, from the mosque, moving upward and outward, the voice of the muezzin caught up with him, announcing the hour for prayer. Around him, the atmosphere was filled with a luminescence that roused the stones and a chanting that awoke the living and summoned the people to prayer.

But Qasim saw no light and heard no chanting. His eyes were filled with darkness and his ears were deafened.

He moved ahead like a blunt, slack arrow, urged by a blunt, slack force. He moved ahead and he moved falteringly until he felt that he was moving in a vacuum. Then he sensed a coldness seizing him from all sides. Then he felt nothing, and was felt by nothing, but he went on to the unknown, as many things move on to the unknown every second.

There is no doubt that the sun did shine after that with God's light and that the city was filled with life and activity. There is no doubt that the people vibrated in their affairs with that same struggle of good and evil dispositions that fluttered in their hearts. There is no doubt that Amuna and her daughter waited for Qasim to return to them as always whenever he went to the river at the end of night.

But their waiting was long and nothing came of it.

The reader might like to know how hope played with them, and how despair took hold of them, and how the vicissitudes of time trifled with them. But the reader does not need me to portray these misfortunes. For it is very easy for him to observe this tumultuous life around him. He will recognize many 'Amunas' and 'Sekinas,' who can be counted not in hundreds or thousands, but in hundreds of thousands or perhaps in millions.

The sun rises for them every day, shining with the light of God. But it does not bring them contentment or joy, nor even the promise of contentment or joy. Night approaches them, obscure, intensely dark, preened by the moon in its various phases and decked with points of light that scatter across the sky. But it does not bear them repose or an expectation of repose. It forces them into a heavy, hateful sleep, in which they suffer abhorrent dreams, depicting the sufferings they undergo in the daytimes of their loathsome lives. The sun pays them no attention when it rises and the night pays them no attention when it descends. Since when have night and day cared for the wretchedness of the wretched and the prosperity of the prosperous?

What is astonishing is that living people—who have been allowed hearts capable of feeling, and minds capable of thought, and souls capable of differentiating between good and evil, who have been granted a well-being that should have turned their attention to the hell of the wretched—that these people go on with their lives as the night and day go on to their ends, caring nought for Amuna or Sekina or Qasim, too caught up in themselves to notice any thing or any person.

Khadija

She did not come from the sky as angels mercifully and soothingly descend to earth. Nor did she come out of the river as the beautiful virgin daughters of the water emerged in ancient times from brooks, rivers, springs and wells. The clouds did not carry her to us, nor was she sent by a star. She was raised in the village in one of its miserable, unhappy families as tens, no hundreds and thousands of other virgins are raised in the cities and the villages.

But she was distinguished from her contemporaries by a face so clear and smooth that it seemed the sun had cast its cloak over it.

No one knew from where she had acquired that gracious, cheerful, radiant, and pure face. For her father's face was sullen, scraggy, and carved with wrinkles. Misery, unhappiness, and hardship had done their work. And her mother's face was an admirable picture of ugliness, if it is possible for ugliness to be admirable.

An oppressive life, a coarse livelihood, and such compelling necessities as drive the wretched to engage in occupations they do not like, and which force them eventually to contend with what they hate—all this had enveloped the faces of the two parents in a painful, thick wrapping of gloom, humiliation, sorrow, imbecility, and stupidity.

She was not distinguished by the radiance and purity of her face alone—these were manifestations of a sublime

51

picture of grace and beauty that perfected all of her body, making it a wonderful, meticulous thing, as though it had been created with as much leisure, fastidiousness, and tolerance as the most skillful sculptor would invest in producing his statue: a magnificent splendor, luring all eyes and hearts.

Her voice, when she spoke, was soft, sweet, clear, and full. As soon as it reached one's ear, it brought to mind that brief moment between the launching of dawn, like an arrow in the dark of night, and the rising of the sun upon the earth, drowning it in light and beauty.

Her voice brought to mind that brief moment that exists between dawn and sunrise, that instant in which there sways a gentle breeze and in which the dew falls like a sweet greeting sent to earth by the sky, bursting with life and energy, that moment when nature awakens, full of energy, yet indolent: the birds sing, the leaves rustle, the branches quiver, and the faint light whispers to the earth that it should awaken and prepare, for the sun's procession is almost arrived.

All this was brought to mind by her voice when she spoke, though she spoke but little. That soft, sweet, clear voice of hers suited her radiant, pure face and her wonderful, smooth disposition. For her personality was most like a musical piece, which pleases not the ear alone but all of man's faculties of sense, feeling, and thought.

People would wonder and always ask, "Where did those two parents, whom nature has marked with unsightliness and ugliness, beget this marvel that has taken to itself the most sublime and purest loveliness?" When people persisted in their disbelief and wonder before the wise man of the village, he would recite the following verse from the Quran, reproaching them for their unending astonishment:

Thou causest the night to pass into the day, and
Thou causest the day to pass into the night.
And Thou bringest forth the living from the dead,
and Thou bringest forth the dead from the living.

And Thou givest sustenance to whom Thou choosest, without stint. (*III, 27*)

Then he would say to them, "Beware! Do not deny that God should grant beauty to ugliness if he penetrates the day with the night and the night with the day. You do not deny that the dark night should break through the discerning day, or that the light of day should be defeated by the dark of night. Why then do you deny that God should grant this Khadija to her mother Mahbuba and her father Sha'ban?"

Mahbuba is a middle-aged woman who goes among the inhabitants of the village to bake their bread. She bakes a special kind of corn bread, thin, round, and broad. She does not know how to make wheat bread.

You see her at the end of night going to this or that house to prepare the dough. And you see her at the beginning of morning sitting before the oven, turning over the pieces of dough with her fast, industrious hands and evening them out into the desired shape with astonishing speed. She thrusts them lightly and gently into the fire and retrieves them, cooked just enough to be tasty to the mouth, palate, and stomach.

And you see her at forenoon, when the day is about to turn, returning to her humble, mean home, carrying her pay of a batch of bread, which she stores and on which she and her husband, sons, and daughters live. They make do with it for many days, perhaps adding this or that kind of fat to it if God sends Sha'ban some fortune, or if some of the wealthy families favor this needy family with some food. If neither happens, then it is bread alone, or bread with something that sprouts from the earth and that short-reaching hands may grasp: onions, radishes, or such greens as the destitute are not prohibited from resorting to in life.

Sha'ban is a man with whom fortune has been miserly. He has inherited from his father a craft that does not allay hunger. He is a humble mason. He does not build those houses made of stone, red bricks, or sun-dried bricks. He builds houses and rooms of thick mud. The mud is gathered, water is poured over it, then some hay is mixed into it. The mixture is then flattened into rough pieces that are added to one another to extend into space and rise in the air, encircling or quartering a narrow patch of land, until the building rises to reach two meters or less, when some palm branches are laid across it. Thus rises a house or a room in which the destitute of the village may take shelter, and which will shield them against a minimum of nature's aggressions.

The village people do not build such houses every day or every week. They build them when they are able to build and when circumstances permit them to occupy houses and rooms, or to build above this or that room, or atop this or that house.

Thus Sha'ban would work perhaps a few days, remaining idle for days or weeks. He would enrich his family with the piasters that his work reaped for him from time to time. He would clothe them if he was able to do so, and please them with some delicacies if his hand could reach any.

And so the children had no alternative but to work when they grew up in order to feed themselves at their place of work, returning to their family with the remainder of what fortune came their way.

Khadija was well rounded. She worked in one of the homes of the wealthy. She would rise with the early morning and spend what energy she enjoyed in serving the members of the house, and would return as darkness fell to spend the night at her parents' home. She was content with this life, smiling through it despite some sadness that dwelt in her heart and infused her spirit. Her tongue did not reveal this sadness when it spoke, nor did her face, when it expressed anything.

She undoubtedly thought of the destitution of her parents and young brothers and sisters. But she did not express these dismal thoughts with any utterance, glance, or movement. She concealed her sorrow as a miser conceals his treasures.

Perhaps this sadness cultivated a faintly bitter note, which echoed in that sonorous, sweet voice, leaving a strange effect on the listener. Perhaps from this sadness there evolved a faint, delicate cloud that traveled across that beautiful, radiant face so rapidly that anyone who beheld her did not notice it, let alone inquire about it.

Her life in that house was a continuous delight and full of lasting contentment, only interrupted from time to time, and for very short instances, by a whisper that begins to herald sadness but dissolves before it accomplishes its task.

The mistress of the house is fond of, and gentle to Khadija, sympathetic to her parents, offering them charity whenever she has the chance, and generosity whenever she is capable of benevolence. She often calls Mahbuba to the house and gives her some light or difficult task, paying her not in piasters, which she would have placed in her hand, but with her old dresses or her sons' and daughters' or husband's old clothes, and with food that she asks her to take to her husband and children, or with gifts on feast days or in days of affluence and prosperity, when such prosperous days are around. She does not stop at that form of benevolence, however, but is keen to keep up her gentleness to the family, and sustain her charity.

One day, from the direction of the cattle-shed in the courtyard, there came to her ears the shouts of a woman, the sobs of a girl, the sound of a stick tearing into a body with ceaseless beating, and the screams of children.

She rushed out of her room to see with dread that Mahbuba had thrown her daughter to the ground and taken hold of her long, beautiful hair in one of her hands, wrenching at it violently, while her other hand rose and fell with a stick, a dry branch usually used to turn the bread in the fire or to take it out.

Not far from this painful scene were set aside two porcelain plates that were the object of Mahbuba's glances and interrogation of the girl, as one hand continued to pull her hair and the other steadily rose and fell with the stick.

The mistress of the house asked reprovingly, "What do I see? What do I hear?"

Then she rushed to Mahbuba and pushed her away from the girl, snatching the stick from her hand, and then to the girl, standing her up and keeping her away from her mother. But Mahbuba continued her moaning and weeping. Then she fell into an hysterical fit of the kind that overtakes such women when they sob vehemently. The mistress had to splash water on her to calm her down.

Mahbuba came back to her senses, and when the mistress asked what the trouble was, she heard words that caused her tears to fall heavily.

·She heard that Mahbuba had found these two plates in a corner of her house. She had no doubt that her daughter was betraying her masters and was stealing things from their home.

That she should steal was all that was needed, for she thus betrayed those who were charitable to her and to her family, allowing them a life that held some measure of contentment and comfort. She could do no more to bring harm to her parents and aggravate their straitened circumstances and the misery of their lives.

Because of this theft that her daughter had committed, their means of livelihood had become strained: she had been sent away from some of the houses where she made bread, and her husband had not been summoned to build or to make bricks for a long time.

"We were wondering about the source of all this hardship. Now we know it! We have a thief for a daughter, one who betrays her masters and smuggles things out of their homes!"

The mistress of the house, having wiped her tears, said, "Be careful! Wait, woman! Your daughter did not steal these two plates. I asked her to take them to you last night, with some food on them, as I always do. I suppose she forgot to bring them back to work in the morning."

"She brought us no food yesterday, and has never brought us any food!" Mahbuba exclaimed.

The story unfolded after a while. It was revealed that Khadija was ashamed to refuse what food her mistress charged her to carry to her parents. And she was ashamed to carry this food to her family. So, when she left with any plates, she discarded what was in them, giving it to any poor people on her way, throwing it to the dogs if she found only dogs on her way, and throwing it in the road if she met neither people nor dogs.

She would then hide the plates in a corner of the house and take them back with her in the morning, smiling and feigning satisfaction, as though she had enriched her family with the fortune she had carried to them.

But this morning she had left in a hurry and had forgotten the two plates. She was only reminded when she saw her mother bringing them and questioning her roughly. Where were they from? From where had she stolen them? Then she did not give her time or wait for her answer, but wrenched her hair with one hand, and flogged her body with the dry branch in the other.

She was seized with anger and started to shout, and the girl was overcome with pain and started to cry. The more the girl moaned, the more her mother screamed.

From that day the mistress of the house understood that Khadija was a servant unlike other servants and a girl unlike other girls. She therefore honored her with her affection, distinguished her with her love, and almost took her as a friend.

In the evening, she related the story to her husband. He felt compassion for the girl and her family, and urged his wife to be good to them, reciting the words of God in His glory and splendor:

> (Alms are) for the poor who are straitened for the
> cause of Allah, who cannot travel in the land (for
> trade). The unthinking man accounteth them
> wealthy because of their restraint. Thou shalt know
> them by their mark: They do not beg of men with
> importunity. And whatsoever good thing ye spend,
> lo! Allah knoweth it. *(II, 273)*

The young men of the village listen to the story of
Khadija and talk of the abstention it portrays such as cannot be found among the rich, and of the rare modesty it
depicts that they do not observe in the attitudes of the people they see, nor even in the stories told to them by their
grandmothers.

They speak of Khadija's captivating beauty and of her
loveliness that enchants the eyes, lures the heart, and
haunts the intellect. The youths keep secret in their hearts a
love, admiration, and desire for Khadija, and make public
their esteem and approval of her. Their desires play all
kinds of games with their minds, and draw their hearts in
all directions.

Then one day there comes forth a suitor from a family
that, though not enjoying too great a share of wealth, is
very far from privation. The family owns cultivated land
not far from the village and cattle that leave their home in
the morning and return in the evening, garnering it much
wealth.

The young suitor is strong, abounding in health, bursting with energy, and pleasant looking. He is talkative, especially when he preens himself and goes to the mosque to
attend the Friday prayer, before returning to indulge in
amusement and conversation with his companions. At
first, Khadija's family cannot believe what they hear. Then
they are sure. They accept after some hesitation due to that
mixture of hope that enlivens souls and fear that mortifies
hearts. For what is there to prevent this wretched family
from finding in this betrothal a relief sent by God, one that
will allow it some prosperity after distress, and affluence

after poverty? And what is there to prevent it from realizing its own destitution, and thus from being apprehensive about becoming related by marriage to a family of wealth and comfort?

But the youth is sincere and loving, and persistent in his sincerity and love. His family values nothing so much as his contentment and happiness. It is sincere and insistent in its sincerity, seeking the means to convince wretchedness to fuse with luxury.

Matters are settled between the two families, but they are not settled in Khadija's heart. She refuses the marriage and abides by her refusal, preferring her life as a servant to the life that beckons her to freedom and self-reliance as well as to the ability to help her parents. She refuses and continues to refuse until she arouses suspicions in her parents' hearts. She would not insist on this refusal unless she had compromised herself and had abused the rights honor has on a girl.

Mahbuba reveals her terrible secret to Khadija's mistress in a tearful voice. But the mistress brings her back to her senses and restores tranquillity to her miserable soul and apprehensive heart.

Relentlessly she pursues the girl, sometimes reasonably and sometimes harshly, until she virtually steals acceptance from her.

The young man's family prepare for the wedding day, and Khadija's mistress also prepares for it. She sets the girl up for her memorable day as middle-class girls are best set up for it. She insists that the wedding procession should set out from her house and not from Sha'ban's.

One night Mahbuba prostrates herself before her humble home wanting to weep but not finding the tears, wanting to speak but not finding the words. Only a mysterious and ugly sound vibrates in her throat, which, if anything, belies her fear and consternation over what one of the hours of the night will expose when the young man enters to his wife.

There she is flat on the ground, her body shaking violently from time to time, a shiver—now light, now violent—running through her limbs, and that indeterminate, ugly sound coming from her throat, while around her, happiness fills the hearts of the youths with delight and pleasure.

Then the ululations are launched like silver arrows breaking through the pitch-black night. Here and there gun shots resound. A group of women and boys appear. They have raised something that looks like a dark red flag, proof of the bride's virginity. They cry out words that are repugnant to the ear and offensive to good taste. The arrows of the ululations fly in succession as though they are attempting to rip the bowels of the night apart.

And an impertinent woman violently shakes Mahbuba and strongly rebukes her, telling her in a loud voice, "Compose yourself! What are you afraid of? Khadija has whitened your faces and brought you honor."

Calm gradually returns to Mahbuba. The women have lifted and seated her, and offered her some water so she can come back completely to her senses and full strength.

The night ends as wedding nights end. Morning dawns the next day, but Khadija appears to the visiting women only because she has to. She listens to everything they say, but tells them nothing and tries to check her tears, but does not find the means to do so.

They ask her, and ask among themselves, what is wrong with her and what is the source of the gloom that overwhelms her spirit and of the tears that drench her face?

Since when do people see a girl's heart full of sorrow on a day when hearts should overflow with happiness and joy? They ask her and receive no answer, because she cannot find the answer within herself, or let us say that the answer is resting in her soul but she cannot reveal it because she cannot reach it or conquer it.

They ask among themselves and find no answer to the question they pose. If they had been left to their natures, they would have invented an answer. For nothing is easier for them than to raise suspicions, truthful or false.

They had seen the girl being led to her husband, pale and pallid, with eyes downcast, containing herself with much difficulty, as though she were being led to death and staring it in the face.

Her mother had been prostrate on the ground, overtaken with that same shaking that besets those suffering an epileptic fit or possessed by the devil. Was there not in all of this, or in part of it, something to arouse suspicion?

But they had seen the dark red flag fluttering in the dark of the night amid the glittering of the lanterns.

Dawn rises, and the day is almost half done, and here is Khadija's mistress come to visit her, bringing her greetings, and a present as well. She sees and hears, and is alarmed by what she sees and hears. She takes the girl aside, where they can be alone for a long time, then comes out laughing and telling those around her, "Child's play and the bashfulness of a naive girl, which the days will soon erase as they do many things!"

But the days pass and erase nothing, although it seems to those around Khadija that the days go by as they usually do after a wedding. For the girl is calm and serene, although her radiant face has lost no small measure of its beauty and gaiety and is clouded by a permanent veil of delicate sorrow that further endears her to the people's souls and enhances her position in their hearts. Through her soft, sweet, clear, full voice there now runs a sad, defeated tone, giving it a more delightful resonance to the ear and a swifter penetration of the heart.

The girl's husband is happy and exultant as husbands are best happy and exultant.

Dawn boldly sets out one day seeking to erase the traces of the night. The earth is immersed in that sweet hour that comes between the first glow of dawn and the rising of the sun, that sweet hour that Khadija's voice used to recall to people's minds, along with the fluttering of the breeze, the rustling of the leaves, the trembling of the branches, the dripping of the dew drops, the singing of the birds, and the awakening of nature.

In that calm, beautiful hour, the women and girls of the village set out for the river, singing of the beauty of life, as though it were a dream that comes to them at the end of their covenant with the night and the beginning of their covenant with the morning.

Then they return to the village, silent, the smiles gradually fading from their lips, a cloud of gloom slowly shadowing their faces, and care, in its various shapes, reawakening in their hearts. They brace themselves to endure the burdens and the pains of life, now that the sun has drowned their village in its persistent, ponderous light.

They go to the river joyous and gay and return to the village with dejected minds and miserable hearts.

A little later in the morning Khadija was missed and could not be found. On the river bank, in a place far from where the women usually filled their urns, they found a full urn and some jewelry beside it.

Khadija was asked of the river but she was not granted.

Drying tears that wanted to flow, and steadying a voice that insisted on breaking, her mistress said, "I forced Khadija into marriage, and it soiled her pure modesty and her chaste soul. Love could not cleanse them, so death did."

Khadija's master said, "And God has punished her parents, for he has written that it should be Mahbuba's destiny to circulate among the houses making bread for the people, and he has written that it should be Sha'ban's destiny that he should never clean the mud off his clothes and hands."

Al-Mu'tazala

In the title of this piece, 'The Isolated Ones,' I do not refer to that famous group of Islamic theologians. Rather, I refer to a wretched Egyptian family that I had forgotten until Egypt was struck by this plague and I was seized by a persistent remembrance of it. I have strained to rid myself of thinking of it, but have failed. I have therefore decided to divert myself by writing about it. Perhaps this narration will transfer it from my personal conscience to the public one. This would alleviate my burden, relieve my anguish, and remedy some of the ills of my soul. For profound troubles are assuaged when they are borne by several consciences rather than weighing on a single one, however strong and forbearing it may be. Imagine, then, if this particular conscience enjoys neither strength nor endurance.

I had intended to dedicate the story of this woeful family to those inhabiting this earth in luxury and ease, not in order to defile luxury for them, but to beautify it in their hearts. Not to turn them away from comfort, but to further entice them with it and to prod them toward it.

Since time immemorial wise men have said that the staunch man should not look to those who surpass him and thus feel his heart filled with ruefulness and his soul weighed by unease. Rather he should behold those who are less fortunate than him and acknowledge the fortune

63

that God has granted him, thanking Him for His gentleness and care, for having bathed him with His grace. He
should therefore cling to whatever good has been meted
out to him and enjoy whatever he has been destined to
possess.

I am the last person to suggest that the affluent should
renounce their affluence and the blessed should disdain
their blessings. Firstly because I know that I would not
succeed in fulfilling such a desire, however strenuously I
should attempt to do so, and however brilliantly I should
embellish my message and adorn my words. Secondly, I
know that the luxury of the affluent comes to them through
God's predestined will and inevitable destiny, and that
there is no means to alter divine will, to change destiny, or
to cancel God's laws for humanity. For God has created
men as we see them, with this differentiation amongst
them: that some live in affluence until they are tyrannized
by affluence, and luxuriate until luxury tires of them,
while others live in privation until privation grows weary
of them, and toil until toil rejects them. Furthermore, and
on top of all these reasons, I dislike being like the fox who
tried to get the grapes. When he failed to do so, he found
fault with the grapes, and claimed that they were unripe
and sour.

It had occurred to me to give this narrative another title:
Umm Tamam, referring not to the wife of our great poet
but to the head of this miserable Egyptian family, who
went by her eldest son's name. It had also occurred to me
to dedicate the story of this mother and her three children
to the miserable and wretched who had been touched by
injury before the plague, and with whom this injury persisted after the plague when death had snatched away their
children, parents, brethren, and supporters, leaving them a
prey to destitution, not knowing the means of either evading or of enduring it, or of being rid of it. I thought of
dedicating this story to them, not in order to cause them to
resent their wretched lives and bleak existence; one must

not cause a wretched man to hate his wretchedness or to despise his misery. Rather one must endear his wretchedness to him so that he may tolerate it and increase it if he can. One should embellish his misery in his heart so that he may be patient with it and immerse himself further in it if he can.

For wretchedness is the inevitable fate of the wretched, just as luxury is the inevitable fate of the luxuriate. Misery is the ordained destiny of the miserable, just as happiness is the ordained destiny of the happy.

The judicious, resolute, and prudent man should be content with predestined fate and inevitable destiny, enduring prosperity without forsaking it and tolerating harm without resentment.

For some reason people of the East have been described as being resigned toward fate, acquiescent to destiny, and subdued in the face of misfortune. Let us at least accept the West's words, opinions, and conceptions of us. Let those living in abundance commandeer the courage to endure abundance and let those living in wretchedness assume the courage to tolerate their wretchedness. Let the rich be patient with their affliction of wealth and the deprived be patient with their captivity in deprivation, until both reach that dwelling place where neither wealth nor deprivation exist, where there is neither poverty nor richness, neither relief nor strain, and where equality among all people is realized once they all are reduced to dust, as they were created from dust.

However it may be, I was faltering between these two titles: *Al-Mu'tazala* and *Umm Tamam*, as I was unresolved as to whom to dedicate this story to—the prosperous or the wretched. In the end I give the reader a choice between the two titles, and dedicate the story to both groups. For the narrative embraces that which is satisfying to both the thriving and the miserable, and what greater and more important a craving can a writer have than to satisfy his readers in their diversity?

And the narrative of this wretched family also contains that which is dissatisfying to both the thriving and the miserable. And what is the value of a writer if he does not dissatisfy his readers in their diversity?

I want always to be a writer of value: satisfying and dissatisfying my readers, pleasing and upsetting them, arousing their admiration until they adore me, and annoying them until they learn to hate me.

I pretend that the affluent should find in the chronicle of this family a story that will endear them to their affluence until they cling to it with their nails (as the saying goes), and until they are delighted with me. I would also like to portray this affluence to them as repulsive and detestable, inveterate and sordid, until they are utterly vexed with me.

I pretend that the suffering should find in this wretched family's chronicle a story that would teach them to be patient with adversity until they are pleased with me, and would instruct their hearts that their life is unbearable and that they are entitled to be transported to a more lenient and gentle one, then comprehend that they have no means of realizing this escape, until they are utterly vexed with me.

I would thus achieve my objective: to satisfy and to vex my readers, however great the differences between them may be. I seek nothing beyond that. I speculate no further. What should I care if the thriving should thrive to death, or if the wretched should be consumed by their wretchedness? I care nothing for that. For I am a man belonging to the age in which he lives, and I single out that trait by which this age is most distinguished: selfishness and egocentricity. I am a selfish man who loves only himself and thinks only of himself and cares only for himself.

I am a writer who is concerned only with manipulating readers with the satisfaction and the indignation I stir in their hearts and the love and hatred I arouse in their souls.

There is nothing I despise more than moralizing. Nothing revolts me more than tempting the rich to show compassion for the poor, or encouraging the wretched to suffer their wretchedness. What have I to do with all of this? I am surrounded by people who do not savor the taste of mutual support or comprehend the value of sympathy. They do not care for each other. And they have no consideration for each other. They do not mourn the pains suffered by others. So why should I assume the burdens that people around me do not want to bear? And why should I plunge into this useless aberration that yields no benefit to anyone? Why should I not follow the trend of this generation and live the life of my contemporaries and learn from Abu al-'Alaa's lines: "And when I found ignorance rampant among the people I feigned ignorance until it was said that I was ignorant."

Selfishness, sir, is the sound foundation on which our admirable social system is based. For it, we sacrifice our lives. We defend it with all the force within our power and beyond it. He who wishes to defend this system, to embrace it, to safeguard it from being tampered with by the mischievous, or from being visited by misfortunes that are undesirable for him and for us, should be selfish to the utmost extremes of selfishness, egocentric to the fullest measure. He should care about others only insofar as they serve his interest, realize his gains and bring him closer to fulfilling his aims. But if he and they are isolated from each other, and if he fails to recognize the secrets of the ties that render him in need of them, and they in need of him, then he need only completely ignore and utterly despise them, going on his way, enjoying the luxuries of life, caring nought for the terrors that embrace them, the worries that overwhelm them and the catastrophes and calamities that are instigated against them.

This is how we live and this is how we should live. The slightest deviation from this mode of life is liable to expose us to many terrors, and crush us with grave worries.

For how could our life proceed smoothly if those living in affluent affluence and ample wealth should attend to those possessed by wretched wretchedness and painful suffering, alleviating some of the misery suffocating them and allaying part of the suffering that consumes them? This would distract the affluent from enjoying their delectations and relishing those bitter-sweet, sour-mellow fruits that they reap from the destitution of the destitute and the wretchedness of the wretched. It would distract them from meeting to enjoy their trivial chit-chat at the approach of noon, their trivial entertainments at the arrival of evening, their trivial frolicking and roistering at the descent of night, and their heavy slumber when the morning resolves to shine.

Life would then lose its splendor and the world be robbed of its adornments. Life in Egypt would be saddled with melancholy and bitter exasperations, devoid of all serenity, forgiveness, and beauty.

Suffice the wretched that our tongues should be kind to them while our hearts avoid them, that we should pity them with words and be intemperate with them in deeds, deserting them to the misfortunes of time and the calamities of their days. Suffice the wretched that distresses should devour them and choke on them, and teach them to savor bitter agony and swallow galling malignity.

I say all this in earnest, not mockery. For God is capable of touching the world with a wing of His mercy and allowing all its peoples to secure the comfort, wealth, and well-being they aspire to. And God is capable of touching the world with a wing of His wrath, imposing upon its inhabitants the misery, wretchedness, and suffering they despise. And since God did not render all people fortunate, and did not create them all unfortunate, but meted out their fortunes in the manner we behold, then it only remains to us—and it is our duty—to exonerate ourselves and exonerate each other from admonition, declamation, and reproach, and to each be content with that share of fortune allotted to him. It is up to us—and it is our duty—to ascertain that the fortunate should realize

God's will on earth and bask in their fortune as intensely as they can, and that the wretched should realize God's will and wallow in wretchedness up to their shoulders and ears, or even up to the hair on their heads if they so wish.

The reader may feel that I have exaggerated in digressing from the subject of this isolated family, and the story of Umm Tamam. But he is grievously wrong if he thinks me guilty of this excess. Even if he were completely justified in judging me excessive, I care nothing for his wrongs and rights. What is important to me is that I do not think I have prolonged my introductions or digressed from the subject of my narrative. I said that this plague that has befallen Egypt first brought back to me things I had forgotten about this isolated family, then it cruelly insisted on coming back to me. I could not reminisce about this family so continuously and persistently that my mind and my heart became observers and analysts, without some thoughts being aroused in my mind, some emotions being stirred in my heart, and some sorrow radiating in my soul.

Masterful writers postpone their minds' reflections, hearts' emotions, and souls' sorrows to the end of their narratives, making of them an example to those who wish to follow examples, and an exhortation to those who seek counsel. These writers portray themselves as authorities on morality and as social reformers. They are completely satisfied with themselves. They do not realize that the reader is more cunning and crafty then they, and that he usually reads only the beginning of the narrative to enjoy whatever entertainment he seeks or may find therein. He discards the ending because he is utterly impatient with sermonizing, instructions, and reform.

And some seasoned writers scatter their minds' thoughts, their hearts' emotions, and their souls' sorrows throughout their work from beginning to end, making of their plots mere wrappings for these sermons and exemplars. They are able to deceive some readers, but they do not deceive all of them. For as soon as the intelligent ones start reading, they discern the writer's craftiness and guile. They then either continue to read reluctantly, or desist immediately.

As for me, I have decided—and continue to declare— that I do not want to educate the ignorant, preach to the unheeding, or rouse the distracted. I have nothing to do with all that, for I am certain that all readers are knowledgeable people who cannot be accused of ignorance. I am sure that they are all intelligent and cannot fall into inattention, that they are all sentient and cannot become distracted.

I have said—and continue to say—that I do not want to deceive anyone. For I do not underestimate my readers, nor do I look upon them as children for whom medicine must be disguised with such refinements as would spare them its bitterness and unsavoriness. Why should I do this when I am not giving them any medicine? For I am not a physician, nor are they ill.

Why should I do so when I am completely satisfied with the life that we lead, when I am entirely at ease with it and have full admiration for it? I do not wish to change any part of it, nor would I like any part of it to change.

The opening of this narrative reveals, I think, very clearly that I am fundamentally conservative, a rightist who despises no one so intensely as the leftists.

For all this, I have chosen to speak to the readers in this article about Umm Tamam and her isolated family. For Umm Tamam portrayed rightist conservatism most wonderfully, truthfully, and potently. She was an Upper Egyptian. Upper Egyptians, as the reader knows, are conservatives. They have not been corrupted by education. Learning has not caused them to deviate from the straight and narrow road. Civilization and its numerous antics have not taught them that injustice exists on earth and must be lifted from it, and that there is justice in the heavens that must descend to earth and blanket it with security, peace, and contentment. They are a people who live according to their instincts and who allow themselves to follow their natural disposition. They found the world a playground for a few angels of justice and many demons of injustice. They grew fond of the former and accustomed to the latter, and asked of both only that they should proceed with their playing. If they were touched with some goodness from this playing, they enjoyed it. And if they were touched by adversity from it, they suffered it, neither resenting nor remonstrating against it, nor attempting to alter it.

It is said that the writer chooses his characters according to his own image. He may actually carve them out of himself. Were it not that Umm Tamam was submerged in wretchedness and misery and quite hideous and unsightly, I would have claimed I had carved her out of myself.

But I am not submerged in wretchedness and misery, and I thank God in all cases. The reader will learn that Umm Tamam's portrait bears no resemblance to me. This will undoubtedly prove to him that I neither invented or imagined her, and that my weak and weary imagination has absolutely no bearing on her life or on her family's life. She is a reality created by God as He creates all realities, and as He metes out among people their share of beauty and ugliness and their share of happiness and misery.

This Umm Tamam was so bizarre in all aspects that I am unable to decide which aspect to start with. Perhaps it would be useful to present you with the bleak, humble image of the bleak, humble house where she and her children lived.

This house was most like a filthy stain that spoils the beauty of a spotless and beautiful dress. It was extremely narrow and low. It had been built of that simple soil that the fellahs mix with chopped straw and hay and flatten tightly, and which is called *tauf* in central Egypt. They then stack some of these *taufs* around a piece of land, raising them toward the sky a little, and extending them in space a little. Then they place a cluster of palm leaves or corn stalks on top and make a door of thin wood. Thus it becomes a home where they seek refuge and shelter from the cold of winter, the heat of the summer, and the rains from the sky, inasmuch as it is possible for such a tottering building to protect those sheltered in it from cold, heat, or rain.

This tiny, humble house of Umm Tamam's stood between two huge, stately houses, or rather between the two spacious courtyards of these two houses. In each of these courtyards trees and bushes grew as though each of them were striving to become a garden in front of the house, but had not managed to attain that status and remained, instead, something between a neglected courtyard and a garden that received a little care from people who sought some repose and diversion therein.

I do not know how this tiny, humble house came to stand between these two stately mansions. I have asked the people around me about this, as I have asked them about how Umm Tamam and her children had come and settled there. I found no answer. For they were all newcomers to the village, summoned as laborers to the Khedive's estates, and because the village itself was new, having been founded by the estates. They therefore knew very little, or less than very little, about their neighbors and their village.

Umm Tamam's comportment and that of her children prevented their neighbors from learning anything about them. For they isolated themselves from the people to an inordinate degree—but the time for discussing this seclusion has not yet come.

You should first become acquainted with Umm Tamam, or at least be able to picture her. Her image is worthy of portrayal: she was unusually short and unusually stooped. Her physique aspired to ascend in space but she failed to stand erect. Her upper half bowed down to her lower half, as though she had been created to cleave to the ground. For this reason she was more like the four-legged

creatures than humans with their straight postures and
upright figures. One imagined therefore that she rolled like
a ball when she walked. And indeed her gait was gentle
and slow, resembling a rolling ball when its driving force
weakens and it slowly wobbles to a standstill.

Umm Tamam's voice was thin and frail. She had lost
some of her teeth so that when she spoke her voice would
be transformed to a faint sound, in which the listener could
distinguish syllables only with great difficulty.

Two sons lived with her in that tiny, humble house of
hers. One of them, Tamam, was almost twenty years old.
The other, Abu al-'Alaa', was a little over fifteen. Tamam
and his brother worked in bricklaying. Tamam did his best
at laying bricks, while his brother carried mud, water, and
other materials used for building. From this sometimes
permanent, sometimes intermittent employment the two
boys managed to earn barely enough to sustain their family.

Umm Tamam also had a daughter of twelve or thirteen
called Sa'ada. Beauty and ugliness were strongly at log-
gerheads over her face and her whole body. Beauty, relying on the vigor of pubescence and youthfulness, wanted
to claim her for itself, and ugliness, relying on wretchedness and the privation that ensues from it, strove to possess her. Between these two enemies, the girl was much
like a ball being tossed back and forth by two players.

No one knew of a head to this family. No one even
knew how it had come to descend from Upper Egypt to
this village in central Egypt. People believed that Umm
Tamam had assumed the task of raising her three children
alone, or practically alone, and had borne much toil and
many ordeals in so doing.

She had come down with them from her own Upper
Egypt to this village after moving between many cities and
villages, staying a year or so in this city, a few months in
that village, then a few weeks in the next, and a few days

in another, until she finally came to rest in this village of ours where she settled down and extended her stay.

Umm Tamam's maiden name was no less strange than the name she was called by or the shape of her body. For if you wanted to pronounce it as the village people used to, you would have called her Sitt Abuha ('Lady of her Father'), and if you were to pronounce it according to the rules of our classical language, you would say Sayyidat Abiha, or Sitt Abiha, as it was pronounced in olden times.

This name sounded strange to us, since we used to utter it as though it were one word, not two, and would wonder what the meaning of that strange word was.

Umm Tamam never attempted, nor did her children ever attempt, to associate with others except when they were inescapably obliged to. For they needed to buy food to stay alive. And Umm Tamam sometimes needed to sell. Sometimes she went out on the public agricultural road and collected cow and ox dung, which she cut up into more or less equal pieces and dried on her roof. She used it for cooking, if she had the means to cook. From time to time she would sell what remained of it to some of the village women for a few piasters, thus giving herself and her children some relief.

To my knowledge, it never occurred to any of the wealthy people or to the people living in the two neighboring houses to favor this family with benefaction—not because the wealthy are niggardly in helping the needy, but because, most probably, they set out to give them alms and their charity was met with aloofness, which is not acceptable from the poor. Thus the wealthy gave up their attempts at kindliness and relief.

The likes of Umm Tamam in the villages sometimes mitigated their lot and that of their children—and sometimes even of their husbands—by working in the homes of the affluent and rich. From this work they earned sustenance for themselves and left-overs and discarded clothing and things they could bring home, where the hungry would eat, the bare would be clothed, and the destitute would savor some of life's delicacies. But Umm Tamam did not attempt anything of this kind, or even think of it.

It seemed, too, as though she had prohibited her children from attempting, as some poor youths did, to associate with the rich and affluent youths. For the boys did not take part in either frivolity or sobriety. Sometimes people would notice them sitting beside each other drawing on the ground or playing *al-tab*, a game of stone counters in the dust. The village people thus looked upon this family as being bizarre, distant, and uncouth. The family was not part of them and they were not part of it. Nevertheless, they would speak among themselves about these people with much compassion, though not without sarcasm and perhaps cruelty, if it is possible for compassion to be cruel. This cruelty was expressed in the form of gloating. They would observe the two boys enduring formidable drudgery and severe hardships to earn a handful of piasters every few days, and they would wonder how this family subsisted on such little earnings. They would observe them in clothes so tattered that they revealed parts of the body that have the right to be concealed. These clothes had been patched so often that they had grown weary of patches. They would see the young girl Sa'ada in her threadbare garments and feel compassion for her blooming maidenhood cloaked so outrageously. They would say to each other, "Were it not for their arrogance, these people would have had an easier and more lenient livelihood."

As for Umm Tamam, she could only be seen enveloped in her black cloth, rolling toward the public roads at sunrise, and rolling back at noon, carrying the dung she had collected. Perhaps people saw her crouching on the roof of her house, cutting and flattening the dung, a hideous scene.

*

The plague strikes when this century is not yet two years old. This village is included among the villages and cities it attacks. The people are devastated by the loss of their children, their relatives, and their loved ones.

Umm Tamam is at the head of those whom the plague devastates. It snatches away her two sons in less than five days. Yet she remains quiet and calm, bowing her whole body to the ground, neither raising her voice in wails, nor lowering it in moans. She stays in her house, where she confines her daughter as though they were waiting for the plague to reach them and snatch them away as it had snatched the two youths.

But the plague has taken its fill from this house and does not return. At the end of Umm Tamam's fruitless waiting, the people watch her and find that her habits have become altogether different. She does not like her house, and does not like to stay in it. Yet she confines her daughter there and forbids her to leave it. She sets out with the rising sun and returns to her house and daughter only when the night has spread its darkness over the earth, and death and sickness secretly creep into the people's homes.

Umm Tamam would leave her house at sun-up, wrapped in her black cloth, bowing her whole body toward the earth. She would pause for an instant in front of her house and face the west, raising her head with great difficulty toward the sky and gazing before her. She would then turn right and left snatching the air into her nostrils, as though she were trying to capture a furtive and faint scent. She was in fact sniffing for the scent of death and determining whether it was creeping to the right or to the left.

Then she would only be seen in one of those homes where death had struck, and where a weeping, wailing vigil was under way. She would arrive there and address no one and listen to no one. She would proceed to the assembly of weeping women and sit wherever she found herself, neither raising her voice in wails nor lowering it in moans nor slapping her face or clawing at her bosom, not behaving like any of the other women. She would sit there motionless and bowed, like a piece of rock that had been hastily smoothed and crudely carved.

Copious tears would flow from her eyes, as though they were small springs that break out of the mountain rocks.

When she had had her fill of crying in this house, she would leave it for another, then a third, and continue thus until the day was over, speaking to no one, barely being spoken to by anyone, and not responding to those who did speak to her.

Was she weeping for her two sons? Or was she weeping over the children of the family she had joined? Or was she weeping for all those felled by the plague? Was she weeping for her daughter and for herself who had not been felled by the plague?

How did she live? How did she manage to keep her young daughter alive? No one was ever able to find out. No one attempted to help her, and she did not seek the help of anyone. She just spent the days of the plague sniffing the scent of death when morning came, shedding her tears in the homes of death during the day, and returning to her home and her daughter when night approached.

The agony of the plague finally retreats. Umm Tamam comes out of her house in the morning, day after day, facing the west and sniffing out the scent of death. But the breeze does not carry it to her. She then retraces her steps into the house and closes the door behind her. The day sees her only when she comes out in the morning to sniff out the scent of death.

Then one day some of the village people see her going out before noon, holding her daughter's hand and walking slowly toward the west. They say to each other, "Umm Tamam has grown weary of her idleness and has tired of this inactivity. Hunger has become unbearable for her and her daughter. They have come out looking for a means of living and some of God's favor."

But at midday some fellahs approach carrying a body that death has consumed, and another that has violently rejected death.

They had seen Umm Tamam trying to drown herself and her daughter in the Ibrahimiya Canal. They had hurried to save them, but while they had reached the young girl in time, death had reached the old woman before them.

The goodly people buried Umm Tamam and sheltered Sa'ada in one house for a few days, in another for a few more. But Sa'ada had come out of the river stupefied, retaining no sense or reason. She became burdensome and taxing on those who sheltered her.

After only a few weeks she is expelled from the houses and homes. She becomes homeless, wandering about as long as she can, and resting when she has to. You would see her in a village street in the morning, in an alley in the evening, and on the public road in between times, walking as slowly as a tortoise or running as fast as a rabbit. Sometimes you would see her sitting on the bank of the canal, gazing at the water as though she wanted to plunge into it, or gazing at the sky as though she wanted to rise up to it.

The people came to recognize Sa'ada the Idiot. And they forgot Umm Tamam. They came to regard Sa'ada the Idiot as village people regard her likes: at times pitying her and mocking her at others.

Sa'ada the Idiot nevertheless continued to live and grow, her body becoming rounded, and her figure straightening. Wretchedness ridicules her by casting a trace of beauty over her face. Yet she is an awkward idiot, incapable of working, incapable of talking. She does not settle down in one place but wanders between the villages. She is seen in this village one day, and in that village the next.

One day the village people saw her and beheld an astounding sight, that should have broken their hearts in sadness and rent their souls with grief and indignation. They beheld this offensive, abominable, and ugly sight, yet it stirred no compassion in their hearts nor did it move their tongues with one word of commiseration. Instead they looked, then laughed among themselves and exchanged those coarse, uncouth phrases that characterize the mockery of village people.

For they see Sa'ada the Idiot walking along with her stomach moving between her hands. She has been abused by one of the road ghouls who has placed a fetus in her womb. She is an idiot who cannot differentiate between a ghoul and a man, nor between an angel and a devil. She does not know what is asked of her nor what she desires—if it is possible for the likes of her to desire.

Where did Sa'ada go with that fetus she carried in her womb? Was it allowed to see light or not? What became of it and of its mother?

I will tell you nothing of this for I know nothing of it. I have told you all I know. For I moved from the village before learning any more about the fetus or its idiotic mother. Then I was distracted from any thoughts of the fetus and its idiotic mother. I forgot Umm Tamam and her two sons, and for forty-five years I moved among those affairs of life designated for me by God.

I return to Egypt after an absence and find the plague here. Suddenly I recall Umm Tamam and her idiotic daughter Sa'ada. Suddenly I ask myself if this new plague could encounter what the old plague encountered in the tale of Umm Tamam and her likes?

It is said that conditions have changed in Egypt, and that life here has improved in the past half century. But these conditions that have changed, and this life that has improved have not prevented the plague from revisiting.

Who knows, perhaps the change of conditions and the advancement of the socio-political system do not preclude the possibility that there should exist in one of the villages of Upper Egypt, or Lower Egypt, or close to Cairo, an isolated family like that of Umm Tamam.

A Comrade

It was one of those hours of forenoon when the day
should have lingered in its stride to cage the youth of the
kuttab, confining them to that life of theirs, submitting
them to the violence of the master and the cunning of the
monitor. It should have lingered to delay that happy mo -
ment when they would be allowed the freedom to have the
lunch they anxiously awaited, not to satisfy their need for
food, but to satisfy their need for liberty and play. The
children and youth of the *kuttab* used to feel that the coming of noon and the decline of the sun was too slow. They
used to divert themselves from the irksome and loathsome
waiting with bursts of a strange and sudden energy: their
voices would rise in reading and the movements of their
hands would accelerate when rubbing the boards to erase
what had been memorized yesterday, and write what was
to be memorized that day after lunch. The *kuttab* then
would be like a beehive, full of movement, activity, and
noise that would rise until it could be heard from far away,
carrying distinctions and variations between the thin, high,
and as yet undeveloped voices of the younger children,
those of the children grown a little older and beginning to
become more full, and the voices of young men that were
more like men's voices and had almost reached complete
maturity.

These different voices, emitted in unison, brought sweet and clear music to the ear, bearing much harmony and fluency like music resounding from big musical instruments when the variety in the quality of their resonance is pronounced. From the intermingling of their differences there emerged a beauty that enchanted the ear and filled the soul with wonder and delight. During these hours of forenoon, and also at a later hour of the day when the muezzin is about to call people to the afternoon prayers, the enthusiasm of the pupils of the *kuttab* would reach its peak. It was not easy for the master or the monitor to restore silence without clapping their hands violently and letting roar from their throats a thunderous sound that caused the boys' ears to ring and startled their souls. The children's tongues would become tied, their hands rendered inactive, and they themselves would be reduced to a dumb silence, a stupid inertia, and a strange brooding.

In one of those hours a man beyond his youth but not yet in old age, stood at the doorstep of the *kuttab*. He had an aura of wealth and high position. This was evident from his elegant clothes and from his face, which emanated confidence and arrogance. He held himself high, and had the demeanor of one who is completely content with himself, perfectly settled in life, fearing nothing, suspecting nothing, and suffering no indecisiveness or vacillation.

Most probably he had at some time been an army officer before renouncing the military life for a civil one. He had shifted to this new life while retaining all, or most of, his military practices and habits. Most probably he was not of Egyptian but of Turkish origin, but either he or his family had adopted Egyptian nationality. He bore on his face something, I do not know what, which indicated that he was not an Egyptian, and separated him to some degree from Egyptians. He aroused in their souls, when they examined him closely, a strange feeling that contained both reverence and disdain.

On his way to the *kuttab*, this man had given his two hands to the two boys walking gently beside him. A thin cloud of sadness shadowed the face of the boy on the right. The second boy, on the left, bore a smile on his lips and a radiant face. Vigor and energy flowed from his body. When the man reached the door with the two boys beside him he gave his greetings. The members of the *kuttab* heard a voice they had never heard before in the village. It was a mighty, wide, lusty voice, so strong that it was no longer necessary for the master and the monitor to clap and bellow. For it struck the students' ears and jarred their souls and minds into a dumb, strange silence.

The voice caused the master to leap as if he had been pushed up. All of a sudden he was standing beside his bench, having neglected in his haste to rise in his usual slow and careful fashion. He returned the greeting with some trepidation and ceded his place in the center to the visitor. The visitor thanked the shaykh for his kind reception and for his invitation to him to sit down. But he refused to enter or to sit down and said in that dreadful, frightening voice of his , "I am new to this town. I arrived only two days ago. I learned that your *kuttab* is the best. I therefore chose to bring my two sons here and to entrust you with their education. This one," and he presented the boy to whom he had given his right hand, "has lost almost all of his eyesight. Give him all your attention and teach him the Quran by heart. I have destined him for al-Azhar. As for the second boy, he is an imp. I feel that he is only fit for going to a secular school. Keep him in the *kuttab* so that he does not forget the writing and reading that he has learned, and have him memorize some of the Quran. Treat him with severity if he refuses to stop behaving like an imp in the *kuttab*, as he behaves like an imp at home."

Then he let out a broad laugh that I suspect terrorized some of the hearts of the young boys. He then stepped forward and took the master's hand, placing it on the shoulder of one of the two boys and said, "This is the

Azharian." Then he removed the master's hand from that boy's shoulder and placed it on the other boy's shoulder and laughingly said, "And this is the imp." Then he said to the master, "As for the Azharian, his name is 'Usman. And as for the imp, his name is Mahmud. Do you want me to leave them with you now? Or would you like me to take them back with me today and have them start coming to the *kuttab* as of tomorrow?"

The master started to answer but the man did not give him a chance. Instead, he said, "I will take them back to-day and they will come to the *kuttab* as of tomorrow. Do not let them out for lunch, as it will be brought to them every day. Do not let them out when you perform the afternoon prayers until someone comes to accompany them home. They are strangers and do not know the streets of the town yet. The house is not close to the *kuttab*."

Then he took his leave with that dreadful and frightful voice of his and turned his back without waiting for his salutation to be returned. I suspect he overheard the laugh-ter that the whole *kuttab* burst into and that neither the master nor the monitor were able to silence until they allowed the students to leave for lunch, reminding them that whoever was late would not have his legs spared their share of that well-known agony that was never less than five floggings and could reach twenty.

Both the master and the monitor were pleased with their day and with the good fortune that God had sent them. For this man was an important official who had come to the town a few days earlier. There was no doubt that he was an old Turkish officer. This was evident in his manner of speech and in his Arabic, which was free of jargon and fragmentation, but which nevertheless failed to proceed to its purpose directly. Rather, his tongue was heavy with the language and he found difficulty in pronouncing its words. The monitor further claimed that the newcomer's wife was a pure Turk who could only speak Arabic with great difficulty and painful effort. When she tried to speak

Arabic, her tongue would twist miserably and she would
render the masculine feminine and the feminine masculine.
She did much mischief to some of the Arabic sounds. He
claimed that the two boys had two sisters who had reached
their maidenhood and enjoyed a share of beauty that only
Turks, or Europeans, whom the Turks resemble, are able
to claim.

The master listened to all this without paying it any attention, as was evidenced when his only answer was, "I
don't think he will pay less than twenty piasters per month
as fees for his sons' education."

That day one boy in the *kuttab* failed to rush out with the
others to have his lunch. He was one of those for whom
lunch was brought to the *kuttab*. He had overheard the father's words to the master, and he had heard the master's
and the monitor's words about the father and his two sons
and the whole family. He took it all in and memorized it.
As soon as he reached home, following the afternoon
prayers, he repeated all he had heard to his mother. He
asked her about this family. She answered with a smile,
"It's the family of the new Superintendent of Police. The
woman and her two daughters will visit us in a while.
Make sure none of them catches a glimpse of you!"

II

It was hardly forenoon the next day when the boy made
acquaintance with his two new colleagues in the *kuttab*.
The master had introduced him to them because he was
fond of bringing together the children of families that enjoyed some distinction, and because this boy had memorized and intoned the Quran well. The master therefore did
not hesitate to entrust him with teaching the Quran to the
Azharian boy, and told him, taking his small hand in his
own and placing it on his thick beard, "I have appointed
you as the representative of my beard, so teach this boy
what you have memorized and do so well. Do not dis-
honor me before his father, the important new official.

Appreciate my having delegated to you a task that I should have undertaken myself or delegated to the Monitor."

The boy felt some pride stirring within him. He has now become a teacher, having been one who was taught. He has become one who instructs recital, having been a reciter. He found joy and delight within himself for having entered into a relationship with these two wealthy colleagues who wore European clothes and a tarboush on their heads (instead of the filthy loose clothes worn by the native students of the town), and who belonged to Turkish families and were not descended from families of tradesmen and fellahs.

He set about his work. He asked his student to recite those parts of the Quran he had memorized in Cairo. Then he took this as an opportunity to ask about the *kuttab*s of Cairo. What were they like? How did the masters of these *kuttab*s deal with their students? What were the doctrines they followed in disciplining their students? What were their methods in implementing this discipline? What instruments did they use in so doing?

He would listen to his words ardently and greedily, almost forgetting this student's education that had been delegated to him, had it not been that, from time to time, he recalled his small hand on the thick beard and the master's coarse voice taking on gentleness and kindness and reminding him that he was charging him with an important task that he should have undertaken himself or should have delegated to the Monitor. This used to bring him back to his purpose and induce him to perform his duty. The lesson would thus be spent on an hour for recital and an hour for conversation.

The relationship between the boy and his two colleagues grew in strength. The three of them would leave the *kuttab* after the afternoon prayers, going together sometimes to the boy's home but most of the time to his two colleagues'.

Their house appeared elegant and luxurious to the boy. It filled his heart with awe and admiration when he entered it. It stood by the canal, separated from the water only by a narrow road on which people and their cattle traveled between the town and the village. Behind its high gate, covered with green vines and victorious flowers, a spacious garden unfolded, extending right and left. The house stood behind it, secure, rising only a little toward the sky, but reaching out in breadth. It had many rooms.

What surprised the boy about this house, filling his heart with enchantment and admiration, was that when he crossed this wide garden and entered the corridor that ran between the rooms, he did not tread on dirt, but walked on ground paved with tiles. It often amazed him to see the servant actually washing and cleaning this surface, instead of sprinkling it with water to settle the dust and prevent it rising.

The boy's heart was also filled with enchantment and admiration to notice that as soon as he entered the house with his friends they would turn right and go to a special room inhabited and frequented by none of the household members save the two boys. It was a room specially designated for them to play in. Many strange and diverse toys had been collected there. Chairs and couches had been placed against the walls for the two boys and any friend playing with them to relax on. They did not sit on the ground or play in the empty areas that stretched before the house. Their play was not exposed to the ridicule of grown-ups or the intrusion of interfering infants. It was a luxurious form of play, in a luxurious room, the likes of which the boy had never seen before.

As soon as the three of them would reach the house and settle in their room, they would be joined by the mistress of the house and one of the two daughters. There would then be polite conversation, delicate tenderness, and amiable jesting. Later the boys would be left to their play, at which they would spend the length of time God wished them to spend, be it long or short.

The mistress of the house was a noble woman. She was a little advanced in age but had attractive features. She spoke sweetly but with a strange Arabic that was extremely weak and tortuously twisted. That twisted, strained and slow talk of hers used to enchant the boy and fill his heart with infatuation. As for the two young girls, the elder, Tafida, spoke clearly and joked charmingly, with broken phrases. When she spoke the listener imagined that she was on the verge of falling asleep. She was nevertheless cunning, possessed of a sharp tongue and a stinging humor. She moved slowly and had little energy.

Her younger sister, Iqbal, was a firebrand of incessant energy. She never stopped moving nor did her tongue ever lie still in her mouth. She had a delightful presence and loved playing. Had the choice been hers, she would never have left the boys nor grown weary of their games. But the house was run in the most meticulous and strict manner, and the two girls were allowed only short, intermittent periods of leisure.

The boy luxuriated in this life for a period. He does not remember whether it was long or short. But one day he notices unfamiliar motions in the house and senses that there is something in the air that has eluded him.

Tafida has become engaged. It is only a few days before people come from Cairo and feasts are held in the house. Then the visitors return where they have come from, taking Tafida with them. The house is thus robbed of a not insignificant portion of its beauty and cheerfulness.

Despite this, life goes on with its continuous calm and wearisome succession. The boy continues to perform his duty in helping his friend to memorize the Quran, playing with him and chatting with him.

Mahmud has been transferred from the *kuttab* to a secular school. With the departure of this imp, the *kuttab* too loses not a negligible share of its cheerfulness.

The boy is now left alone with his friend and student 'Usman, teaching him and playing with him. Then weariness comes between them. The boy gradually abandons him, becoming increasingly involved with other friends from the town who introduce him to new forms of play, draw him into pleasant topics of conversation, and read books with him that are unfamiliar to (and do not interest) the children of the *kuttab*. The boy nevertheless continues to meet his affluent friends, sometimes in his own home, at other times in theirs.

One evening he overhears his parents discussing, with some sadness and also with some sarcasm, the fact that the old Turkish officer had left for Cairo, where he had stayed a few days, and from where he had returned in the company of a Turkish woman. She was thirty years old, boasted a charming loveliness and sublime beauty, and had a great influence on the elderly officer. They said that the affluent, elegant house that had been a paradise of bliss had now become the home of sorrow, wretchedness, and misery. It had become an inferno where the mother of the children was being scorched by the flames of anguish, despair, and jealousy and where the three children suffered from witnessing their mother's anguish, despair, and endless weeping. She confined herself to her room, leaving it only when she was compelled to. The children also suffered from witnessing the exquisite bliss in which the officer basked with his young wife in one end of the house.

In the beginning the couple would conceal their happiness and rejoice behind closed doors and drawn curtains.

But happiness carried them away, until they went overboard. Most probably it was the misery of the miserable that emblazoned the happiness of the happy. It was as though this happy couple had noticed the confinement of the recluse, her incessant weeping, and the frowning and

gloomy faces around them and had sensed the quieting of
those voices that used to fill the house with joy and gaiety,
the becalming of those movements that used to fill the
house with happiness and cheer, and had interpreted all
this as a protestation against the happiness they had been
allowed, and a disavowal of the bliss they had been ac-
corded. They accepted the challenge, revealing what they
had concealed and proclaiming what they had kept secret.

Their happiness now appeared insolent, and excessively
so. It showed no reserve and no modesty. It pretended no
sobriety. At first it had crouched in this or that corner.
Then it applied neither stealth nor disguise, but was exchanged by the two spouses before the miserable girl, in
view of the two unhappy boys, and not far from the
wretched mother. Then insolence surpassed its boundaries. The loving couple began to hurt the anguished
woman deliberately. They would jump at opportunities to
display their unsightly happiness, which boasted neither
reserve nor modesty.

One day people speak of that wretched mother being
taken ill, no longer leaving her room or her bed. Then the
news arrives one morning that she is dead. She has been
given relief and found rest, and has left in the children's
hearts an anguish, what an anguish!

This wretched mother is placed in her grave across the
Nile. The master of the house sits to receive those offering
their condolences, as is the custom.

The first nights go by as nights of vigil usually go by:
the people come, shake hands, and listen to the Quran.
One gathering leaves and is succeeded by another. The
recital of the Quran is concluded almost halfway through
the night.

The following day arrives and brings with it the reciters.
The people arrive to offer their condolences and to listen
and to sit in conversation. This they were doing after the
afternoon prayers had been performed, when a young
woman came out of the house and stood amid the assem-

bly, calm and unruffled. She was bare-faced, having neglected to hang a veil over her face. She carried a small bag in her hand. When she took her position in the middle of the gathering the people were dumbfounded. The master of the house tried to get up, but shock had overtaken him and fixed him to his place.

Tafida's voice rose, calm and unruffled. The reciter paused in his recital and the gathering listened to her, frozen, as though a bird were perched on their heads, as she said, "Whoever thinks that he has come to offer his condolences and to be courteous should reexamine himself and his intentions. This is not a night of vigil but a celebration of delight and rejoicing. This man you are consoling has killed his wife and rejoiced in her death. He showed no regard for his maiden daughter's modesty and paid no heed to the young age of his two sons. Instead he scorned all that for the sake of enjoying his new wife. He cajoled and frolicked with her and gained openly from this cajoling and frolicking what a noble and chivalrous man gains only covertly.

"I was in Cairo and knew nothing of this. When I came to bury my mother I heard of it. My ears denied, and my heart disbelieved. But I bear witness, and call upon all of you to bear witness, that I have seen—and my maiden sister and two young brothers have seen—this man frolicking with his young wife and cajoling her, pleased, enraptured, and happy, when only a day or two have passed since the burial of our mother. If you still feel that this man is in need of your condolences, then stay. Otherwise leave now that you are the wiser."

Then she turned away from the assembly. She did not reenter the house but made her way to the station to catch the train that would carry her to Cairo.

I do not know what took place among the assembled group after that scandal, but I do know that the reception of condolences did not last for the customary three days, that the elderly Turkish army officer was only able to stay in the town long enough to prepare for his departure, and that he left one day taking with him the bliss and the hell that surrounded him. All ties and connections between him and the town were severed. The people of the town heard no more of him, and he heard no more of them.

III

Life went on, calm and tranquil, toying with the people and the people trifling with it, its current events effacing the traces of mishaps that had passed.

The boy's family migrated from the town to the upper regions of the country. Other families migrated to lower regions. Each family was distracted by its own affairs from the affairs of other families. Each member of the family was distracted by his private affairs from those of his relatives.

Years passed, followed by more years. The boy became a youth after experiencing the pains of many misfortunes.

One evening, between classes at the old university, he feels a hand on his shoulder and a voice in his ear and this sentence touches his soul: "Don't you remember me? I was at the *kuttab* with you. Have you forgotten the 'imp'?"

No! I had not forgotten the imp. Far from it. He had oc-cupied a very special part in my growing heart that neither his brother nor his sisters occupied, and which none of the comrades of childhood did—those comrades I knew in the *kuttab* and outside it, those with whom ties of friendship had developed in the days of my childhood, whether my association with them was long or short. No—I had not forgotten the imp. More than once, after I arrived in Cairo, seeking an education in the Holy Azhar, I told myself it was possible that I should meet him or his brother and re-vive those ties of friendship that had faded, and link those that had been severed. I told myself that I could transfer a piece of my childhood in the town to Cairo, where I would maintain and nourish it. I would find contentment of heart,

pleasure of spirit, and happiness of mind in the mainte-
nance and nourishment of this childhood.

But I attended al-Azhar for years and years. I became acquainted with many boys, youths, and old men without
finding the imp or his brother, without hearing anything of
them. I could not bring myself to ask about either of them.

Had I asked, it would have been possible to reach the
Azharian I used to monitor in the memorization of the
Quran in my childhood days and, through him, to reach
his brother the imp. I could not bring myself to ask. How
seldom could I think of bringing myself to ask! How often
timidity prevented me from inquiring!

I spent a year, a second year, and a third at the university. I met there students who had studied at al-Azhar and
others who had studied in the secular schools. More than
once it occurred to me to ask about the imp. What news of
him, and where could he be? But I could not bring myself
to ask.

I kept a place in my heart for his memory, which I
would recall to myself, time and again, and which I
reserved only for him and revealed to no one. Until he
approached me one evening and his hand touched my
shoulder and his voice reached my ear and his soul
touched my soul.

We resumed in our youth the life we had lived in our
childhood.

He was new to the university, entering his first year
when I was in my final year. We would meet in the morning, not in his house (for how far were we from that
house!) but in that modest room in which I took shelter
during my days as a student. It never occurred to him to
invite me to his home, and it never occurred to me to ask
him about it.

I started once to ask him about his brother and sisters but
he answered me in monosyllables. When I asked for
more, he dodged my questions and moved to another

subject. I sensed that he was ashamed of his family. I did not ask him about them again.

He had graduated from one of the French schools, obtained the Thanawiya high school diploma, and entered the university. I was trying to learn French. To that end I exerted confused—very confused—efforts, some of which were successful, some of which were not. He loved translating from French into Arabic. He would read me some of his translations and whatever I wanted to learn from French literature.

I may forget many things but I will never forget that he read me *Candide* and the fables of La Fontaine.

I try to remember how we spent the beginning of the night after leaving the university on one particular day, and where we spent it, but I am at a loss. I do remember, however, that I sent my attendant away and stayed with him under the agreement that he would take me home after we had finished whatever we had intended to do. I do not know what it was that we intended to do, but I do know that it was midnight and we were far from my home and close to his in one of the more modest districts, when in a breaking voice he said, "Let's spend the rest of the night together. We can read for as long as we manage to stay awake then you can go home at noon tomorrow."

I agreed to his suggestion. We roamed through winding alleys and reached a humble, dilapidated house. Here we retired to a miserable room where a tattered straw mat was spread and on which a comforter and pillow were laid.

In that room he read me a large part of *Candide*. We did not sleep until two-thirds of the night had passed. The next day at noon I went home and kept him with me until the day's end.

That night I understood the source of that shame that kept him from telling me anything about his family.

The summer months, during which the students are separated from one another, passed. Then came autumn, when they meet. I met my friend among others, but it was a short encounter. For I left for France in the autumn of that year. I said goodbye to him at the train station.

I testify that I did not forget him during that year I spent in France. I testify that I returned to Egypt when the university recalled us before we had completed our studies, thinking that I would find consolation in my friend for the studies being interrupted.

But I arrived in Cairo and asked about my friend and learned that typhoid fever had delivered him to death during the summer.

I do not wish to portray the sorrow and devastation that overwhelmed me. I have not written this story for any of that. But I do remember that one day, after performing the afternoon prayers, I went with two friends to the Megawarin cemetery, where I had been told that he was buried. My two companions and I spent a long time and great effort trying to find his grave to pay our respects to him and place some flowers on it. We could not find it. We returned in despair, having paid our respects to all the graves, and placed the flowers on some unknown tomb.

I was depressed, brooding, and silent. One of my friends, attempting to console me, recited the ancient Arabian poet's words:

> At the graves my friend blamed me for weeping
> And he said, 'Do you weep at each grave you
>   encounter
> for a grave that lies somewhere between
> Al-Lewa and al-Dakadik?'
> Said I to him:
> 'Grief bears grief forth.
> Leave me be,
> for all these are Malek's grave!'

Safaa

"That was possible in those bleak days. As for now, God has made things easier and has made it possible to leave the darkness of misery and wretchedness for the light of leisure and ease. I don't like to go into this matter, nor do I like you to."

Hanena started to respond, but her son Nasif turned his face away from her and moved aside. He lit his cigarette haughtily, rose with deliberate arrogance, and walked out of the room and out of the house as though he had left no one behind. Hanena remained, quiet and dismayed, then dried tears that she would have preferred to let flow, and pulled herself together. She decided that she would talk to her son of this matter again. She got up and started her housework as though nothing had occurred between them.

I have fulfilled, I suppose, what a writer must fulfill when he wants to start a consequential or inconsequential story. I have presented the readers with an obscure paragraph in which neither the subject nor the object appears until the end.

I have done so to rouse in their souls an ambiguity that invites curiosity. Then after this paragraph I mentioned the names of Hanena and her son Nasif to intensify their curiosity. I then separated the mother from her son in a strange, furtive manner. Between them lies this conversation that the son does not want to continue but that the mother is anxious to pursue.

The conversation touches on the hateful past from which the family has emerged, a past any remnants of which the boy wants the family to forget, and which the mother wishes to be loyal to and to protect. This is made evident when she dries her tears and vows to resume discussing it when she sees her son in the evening or at dawn. It is most probable that she would prefer to speak to her son in the early morning when he sits down to his breakfast, calm, relaxed, and clear-minded, when he has not yet undertaken any of his day's tasks or had a chance to remember any of yesterday's. That would be better than talking to him in the evening, when she rarely has a chance of being alone with him.

He usually comes home in haste, has some food with the family, then hurriedly leaves to meet his colleagues and friends. He spends half the night pleasantly chatting with them, then returns when sleep has spread its wing over the whole family and drowned it in a deep lethargy.

The reader is entitled after all this to become acquainted with Hanena and Nasif and their family. He is entitled to learn of this bleak past of which the boy is averse to pre-serving any remnants and parts of which the mother is anxious to save.

I have no objection to granting the reader his rights in this matter if he should accept to travel with me in both time and space. I do not ask him to move with me to a time that is too far removed or to a place that is excessively distant. Rather, I wish to return to the beginning of this century, and to leave Cairo for one of the towns of central Egypt.

For each story there must exist a time and a place that either the writer chooses or that the incidents themselves appoint. I assure the reader that I did not choose, and could not have chosen, the time and place of this story, as I did not choose, and could not have chosen, its characters or incidents. Rather, the nature of things chose these characters and the nature of things caused them to experience those incidents that occurred. The nature of things also chose that this story should take place toward the end of the last century and the beginning of this one. It chose that I should witness this story and be violently and deeply affected by it, and that for some reason of which I am unaware, I should retain it within me. I am now starting to recognize the reason as I begin to dictate this narrative. I witnessed and retained it in order to talk of it to the reader of this book almost half a century after it took place.

I could even assert that I did not choose, and could not have chosen, to take this story as the subject of this narrative. It is rather the story that chose me as a medium through which to reach the reader. I am unable to reveal the reason for this because I cannot—and the reader himself cannot—ask the story why it chose to be advertised now, and why it chose to be advertised through me and through these pages on which I write.

I remember that I spent days and days preparing a topic of French literature, studying and researching it as the subject matter of this article, and that I accomplished most, if not all, of what I wanted and sat by my friend to dictate what I had decided to dictate.

But my friend heard from me nothing remotely pertaining to French literature. Rather he heard the beginning of this narrative. He attempts to contain me, as Hanena attempted to contain Nasif, but I turn my face away from him, and move aside and light my cigarette haughtily and continue dictating, while he is obliged to continue writing.

The characters of this story rise before me, crowding each other, violently insistent, each of them demanding to be rushed to his position in the narrative as though they have been dormant for so long that they have grown weary of sleep, and as though oblivion has weighed so heavily upon them that they have become intolerant of it. They wish to awaken, and they wish me to be reminded of them, and they wish the readers to remember them, and they wish to thus retrieve some share of life, although that former life of theirs was too contemptible and wretched to justify that its victims should contemplate it or should seek to retrieve the smallest part of it.

These characters are quite numerous. I must therefore apply some strict system to put them back in order, and to reveal them only in those places allocated to them in the narrative. I did not choose these places for them. They were chosen for them by their former lives. The characters compose two rural Coptic families who lived next to each other, this proximity establishing the usual friendship and familiarity that grows between neighbors, as well as an easygoing and constant companionship and intermingling and a sharing of life's delights and pains, of its pleasures and displeasures, of such events as occur, misfortunes as transpire, and calamities as befall.

The family of Muqaddis Mikhail Tadrus lived in a house that was neither excessively spacious nor excessively small. It was a medium-sized home, composed of a few rooms that displayed neither wealth nor adversity nor anything remarkable. It was modest but not paltry. It stood at the beginning of the street, alongside the canal, on an easy slope that cost those going to it little exertion. They would descend to it if they approached it from one side and ascend to if they approached from the other, but would not have a difficult walk in either case.

This Muqaddis Mikhail was the owner of a simple trade. He had taken a store some way from his house, where he sold such trash as those beads from which the poor make necklaces and with which the women and girls adorn themselves, and that colored glass from which they make bracelets and hollow circles into which they insert their arms. They would dazzle themselves and dazzle the men with their bright colors and pretty ringing. He also sold the cheap materials that the rural women make their clothes with when they wish to be modest and their refinements when they wish to display their charms.

His shop was especially well known for those embroidered head bands that the women used to wrap around their heads, enticing the men and charming the eyes of the youths.

Muqaddis Mikhail gained from his simple trade enough to provide his family with a life that was, although not completely leisurely, nevertheless not completely strained. It lay somewhere in between, allowing the family to conceive of itself as belonging to the middle class and to aspire to such ambitions as this class aspired to—which, at the time, were extremely modest.

The family was not large. It comprised Mikhail and his wife Hanena, their son Nasif and their daughter Safaa. Clearly, this last name was pronounced not in the classical form in which it appears here but with a short instead of a long 'a.' When uttered, those hearing it suspected that it was borrowed from those metal braids that women used in their hair and hung down their backs and from which a pleasant jangle came whenever they moved.

Mikhail aspired to raise his son above the position that had been ordained for him in life. He therefore did not bring him up in the art of trade so that he could succeed him in the store when old age disabled him, but sent him instead to the secular school, after he had attended the Coptic *kuttab* for one year and part of another. He resolved not to be satisfied with the primary school, but to send his son, if he could, to Cairo to attend school there. He could then become a government official and follow a new career, different to the one Mikhail and his father before him had followed.

Hanena also aspired to raise her daughter above the position that had been ordained for her in life. She therefore sent her to the teacher to whom middle-class mothers used to send their daughters to learn the arts of embroidery and ornamentation and fastidiousness in cutting out and designing clothes.

The boy attended school and the girl went to the teacher, and the family was content with itself and its manner of raising its two children for years. The boy earned his primary certificate after some effort, and the girl took in all that she could of the teacher's art. The family found that it had to send the boy to Cairo and to keep the girl at home. God is witness to the pains Mikhail undertook to arrange for the expenses the boy needed, and to the grief Hanena endured in her separation from her only son. The boy was enrolled in a secondary school where he remained for the time that God wished: a year, and another, and another, without succeeding. Instead he remained in the first grade year after year. The school had to dismiss him. He enrolled in the Greater Coptic School, which at that time accepted boys whom the governmental schools had dismissed for their failure, or whose age precluded their acceptance in other schools, or whose parents' hands fell short of paying the fees for the state schools but whose aspirations were nevertheless far-reaching and who were loathe to think that their children should discontinue their education before earning the secondary certificate, after which they could perhaps find a place in one of the higher schools or obtain employment in an office.

Nasif stayed in the free school a year, and a second, but he failed there as he had failed in the government school. The expenses weighed heavily on his father, and grief weighed heavily on his mother, and the boy grew impatient with his father and his mother and with himself as well.

Then finally he suggested to his father that he should transfer from secondary school, for which he was not suited, to another form of education that would be easier and more attainable and would not require too much culture or too much effort or time. Rather it would take a year or less, after which he would apply for the examination, obtain the diploma, and become a government employee. Thus it was that he enrolled in the telegraph school. Less than a year later he applied for the examination and gained the success he had sought, returning to his family with the diploma, which he had elegantly bound and placed in an elegant tin box.

The father kept gazing at the diploma, trying to read it, and the mother kept gazing at the box admiring its decoration.

The parents quarreled a little about who would keep the tin box. Was the woman to slip it among her clothes or was the father to hide it in one of the drawers of his old desk?

What is important is that Muqaddis Mikhail had reached his limit. He had spent more than his trade yielded and borne more hardship than his years could bear. For the boy's sake he had sold all his wife's humble jewelry, and had obliged his family to bear a loathsome, suffocating poverty that would have been unbearable were it not for the reprieve of hope. No sooner had the boy attained success than the old man was obliged to stay at home and await his livelihood from the scant wages meted out by the state in those days to telegraph officials who were new to their posts.

The government was really frugal in those days. Someone with a diploma would be attached to one of the telegraph offices on a trial basis as a trainee. During this period he would be paid three pounds a month. His salary would not be calculated in gross but on a daily basis not to exceed ten piasters. He was not free to choose the telegraph office in which he would work. Since when have state employees and officials been free to choose the offices in which they work? Rather the state sent employees and officials wherever it wished and wherever the system required that they be sent.

The young man was sent to the furthest regions of Upper Egypt. He would collect his pay at the end of the month and send half of it to his family for their livelihood, and spend the other half on himself. He came to learn, and his family came to learn, that peoples' dreams are not always faithful and often deceive them.

For the young man had obtained his diploma, and secured a government post, and become a distinguished member of a distinguished class, the class of state employees. Yet he was still poor, miserable, and needy, and his family remained a middle-class family being dragged further toward poverty day by day and driven further toward distress year by year.

Distinction costs its bearer much money. For the young man had to adopt a suitable lifestyle among his colleagues. He had to take on the trappings that befitted his class, and lead a life that will not be regarded with disdain or pity by his colleagues.

All this exhausted and constrained him. Sometimes it obliged him to neglect to send his parents the money he was used to sending them, or to send a reduced sum.

This would vex and sadden the family. For its need of a suitable lifestyle was no less than that of the young man. He is alone, while they are a family of three persons. By right, therefore, they should receive the greater portion of the wage, while the smaller portion should be enough for him. How then could he send only the smaller portion? How then could he send nothing?! Had they not consecrated their lives and all their efforts, and all that they owned for this young man's sake? Behold how children disown their parents' rights! Behold how the youth are ungrateful to the elderly! Behold how growing young men covet well-being and luxuries for themselves, leaving their fathers, mothers, brothers, and sisters to suffer from a shortage of funds and substance, nay to suffer misery and hunger and deprivation!

Thus after the son had passed his exams and obtained a position, the family was reduced to poverty for many years, during which they tasted a material and moral wretchedness that they had not tasted when he had been a boy attending primary school, or an adolescent attending school in Cairo.

The second family was that of Mu'allim Yunan. Its head was a humble clerk in one of the Turkish estates. He spent his day bent over his books, doing accounts with the bailiff, or supervising his assistant. He returned to his family at the end of the day content with himself, but tired and weary. As soon as he had had some food with them, and chatted with his neighbor a little, he would go to his bed completely exhausted.

As soon as the morning breathed it would see him on the public road going to work in the office or in the fields. The wage he made for this drudgery was small and paltry, barely sustaining his family of three: himself, his wife Morgana, and their son 'Abd al-Sayyid.

Mu'allim Yunan was a modest man who neither raised himself above his social position nor aspired to raise his son above it. He sought to teach his son his own profession so that he should become a clerk in the estate as he himself was, and as his father before him also had been. His greatest ambition was that his son should successfully learn from him and follow his example until he reached his adolescence, when he would be able to help him in his work, and until the superintendent of the estate might notice him, and perhaps be pleased with him, have pity on him, and pay him a few piasters per day, which would help the family to endure the burdens of life.

But the boy was not kind-hearted, nor was he fond of working. He was dull and lazy, preferring to play when he had a chance or, if he could not play, to lead a lethargic life, more like a daze than anything else. This vexed and displeased his father and sometimes drove him to be hard on the boy. But he was his parents' only child, so the Mu'allim was rough with him only to compensate him afterward, harsh only to be kind later.

Age takes its toll on the Mu'allim until he feels too weak to bear his burdens. But the youth is slow and sluggish in learning his father's trade. When the old man is finally obliged to stay at home, the boy is too ignorant and too lazy to take his father's place. The estate only keeps him on out of consideration for the father's rights and in kindness to his family, according him only half the wages it had paid his father.

Morgana is obliged to leave her home and to work a little to sustain her old husband and help her lethargic son. She starts to go to the nearby villages and buy from their inhabitants the cheese and butter they wish to sell. She carries a huge wooden tray covered in green, damp grass that keeps the cheese and butter moist and makes them enticing to behold. She circulates among the houses selling the cheese and butter, making enough profit to meet her husband's and her son's needs.

The two neighboring families moved along the same path toward distress, then toward intense distress, then toward absolute destitution and privation. Along this path their relationship grew stronger. The two retired old men devoted themselves to idleness and conversation.

Morgana and Hanena began meeting when morning shone, and at the day's end, to borrow utensils and help each other in sustaining the burdens of life, or to exchange gossip. Safaa (with her long or short 'a') started to meet 'Abd al-Sayyid as he left for work on the estate and as he came home. Such empty chats would take place between them as take place between adolescents and as lead to nothing and signify nothing, but which distract them from themselves and divert them from their aspirations.

But the boy is cunning and clever, taking advantage of opportunities and craftily advancing his cause. From time to time he insinuates into these empty chats what he would like to fill them with. In the beginning he is unable to do so—but he does not recognize inability, nor despair, nor failure.

He is insistent and persistent. Success sometimes eludes him, but this does not stop him from renewing his attempts. To reach his end he follows various convoluted paths well known only to those whom life has put to the test, and who have learned from experience. And where is one to find young people who try to run away from the tests of life and the revelations of experience?

A word is uttered by Safaa, and youth injects an unfamiliar sweetness through it and causes it to touch unfamiliar territory in 'Abd al-Sayyid's ear and heart. 'Abd al-Sayyid makes a movement, and youth suffuses it with an unfamiliar gracefulness and causes it to fall on unfamiliar territory in Safaa's eyes and heart. Then is the youth enraptured by that sweet word, wishing it to be repeated and supplemented by others of its like. Then is the girl enraptured by that graceful movement, wishing it to be repeated and supplemented by others like it. Then is each enraptured by the other when they meet and when they part, when night falls and when morning dawns. Then is this encounter—which had been almost accidental and unintentional—now become something for which plans are made and toward which means of arranging it are sought. Then is that chat between them—which had been almost empty and which had concealed nothing—replete with many things. Then do the two families begin to notice that there is something about these two young people. In the beginning they neither object nor approve. Then the elderly hearts smile at this budding relationship between the two youthful hearts. Then Muqaddis Mikhail speaks to Hanena, and Mu'allim Yunan speaks to Morgana—yet neither family says anything to the other. Each waits for the other to broach the subject.

Youth cares nought for the notions brewing in the elders' souls or the thoughts agitating in their minds, but proceeds toward its end, looking not behind but ahead, forever forward. Then it attracts to itself and to the ties it has drawn not only the attention of the two families, but also that of other neighboring families. Here the elders are warned, and Morgana speaks to Hanena and the Mu'allim speaks to the Muqaddis, and the engagement becomes a decided and agreed-upon affair.

Nasif lives in his exile being hurled among the towns of the upper and the lower regions of the land. He has become permanently appointed in his position, no longer receiving his wages on a daily basis. He has become an official in the true sense. His pay has increased until it has reached four and a half pounds, from which his pension is deducted at the end of the month. Nevertheless, his pay has been increased. But it is not only his pay that has increased—his expenses have also risen, as well as his living costs, since he is now a permanent employee. His pay has increased, but his parents' share has not, and remains as it is. Sometimes it reaches them complete, sometimes it reaches them incomplete, and sometimes it fails to reach them altogether.

The boy comes to visit his family during an official holiday. The town witnesses a graceful, elegant youth whom it does not recognize. It witnesses a refinement and comeliness that it does not observe among its own youths, the children of farmers and tradesmen. The head of the Muqaddis is raised with pride when he observes the peoples' admiration and kindly reception of his son, the crowding of the women and girls to see him when he passes through the streets and alleys. The young man is filled with vanity and pride when he sees the people crowding round him, dashing toward him, some of them greeting him from close by and some from afar, and all admiring him, yet all recognizing some arrogance about him.

Some people disapprove of this arrogance in their hearts and some disavow it with their tongues. The father and mother fear for their son from the evil eye of the envious. They yearn for him to stay a long time so that they may bask in his company, yet they equally yearn for him to hasten his departure so as to deliver himself from the malevolence of the malevolent and the evil eye of the envious.

The boy returns to his work after a few days, satisfied with himself, and his parents satisfied with him, and the majority of the townspeople satisfied with him, while a minority are vexed.

It was as though he had come to the town for this short visit in order to bid his father farewell and to see him for the last time. For only a few days after his departure the Muqaddis feels that weakness that old men feel, but hardly pays it any attention. Yet the weakness increases and persists. The old man grows weary and is obliged to confine himself to his home, then to his bed, and then to part with this world.

So the young man returns once more to the town, sad and dejected. Yet sadness and melancholy serve only to enhance his grace and elegance, his allure for people's hearts, and his acquisition of their love and sympathy. For they have done away with much of his gaiety and cheerfulness, his arrogance and disdain, and have subdued him to a certain amount of poise and moderation of humor.

He was a little awed by the realization that, after his father's death, he had now become a man who must assume responsibilities and perform duties. He faced them well: he surrounded his mother and sister with much compassion and care. He diligently and assiduously strove (and sought the mediation of others in securing) a transfer from the distant town where he worked to this town where his family lived. He became an employee in the city telegraph office, living with his family and caring for them, and taking his father's place. The family's life continues in this manner as it would wish, or as it is best able to. For the young man has settled in his home and in the midst of his family.

He is now able to manage his affairs more successfully than he used to when he was away. A better life than had been previously allowed him and his family is now possible.

Many times Hanena wished, as though wishing were fruitful, that the Muqaddis would come back to share this life, enjoy it, and find delight in seeing his son setting off to work or coming home, in his fine uniform, with that handsome carriage of his, and that appearance that fills hearts with admiration and satisfaction. The young man now develops ties with his colleagues in the telegraph office and with others employed at the train station and other groups of employees working at the courthouse or in the post office. He has now actually raised his family to that position of distinction that his father had aspired to for so long. He is now distinguished among those distinguished employees when they meet at the end of the day or at the beginning of the night in that Turk's café that stood on the banks of the canal near the station, and where the employees, especially the younger ones, would go when dusk was at hand, and where they would sit happily and light-heartedly until late at night.

One morning the young man is having his breakfast, his mother beside him gazing at him with admiration, and his sister Safaa attending to him, going and coming, serving this dish and removing that, when he manages to maneuver his sister out of earshot and to be alone with his mother. He discloses in rapid whispers that his colleague has asked for his sister's hand in marriage, and that he approves of this match, perceiving further promotion and increased prosperity in it. For this colleague is a noble son of a noble family. He has lost both his parents and is therefore his own master, collecting the same salary as his own at the end of the month. The young man would like to have a brother, and if the suitor were accepted and the couple were to be married, he would live with them and his mother would gain a second son. The two salaries would be joined, and the family would be flooded with such comfort and prosperity as it could not have dreamed of.

The mother listens to these words and they arouse a strange reaction within her heart, a mixture of great temptation tinged with much sorrow, fear, and regret. For her daughter is already engaged, or practically engaged, to her young neighbor. Her husband has gone to his final resting place acknowledging this match, satisfied and happy with it. In her daughter's soul there is something for this young neighbor—of that there is no doubt. The old lady comes to herself after a doubtful pause and tells her son in a quiet, composed voice, "I wish that could be, my son. But your sister is practically engaged. Our neighbor, 'Abd al-Sayyid, has fallen in love with her and she seems to love him. Your father and I discussed their engagement and your father accepted it."

As soon as the young man hears his mother's words he is consumed with his own arrogance. He answers his mother with the voice of one who has been angered and is about to lose his composure.

"That was then, during those bleak days. But now I don't like to go into this matter, nor do I like you to."

Then he lights his cigarette haughtily and rises with deliberate arrogance and walks out of the room and out of the house as though he had left no one behind.

Hanena bade herself be patient with this unpleasant incident. She did not speak of it to her daughter, and vowed to bring the subject up with her son again. This she did again and again, but she won no concessions from him and encountered only disdain and refusal, until one day he warned her that if she did not obey him he would move out of the town as he had moved into it, and would resume his estranged and lonely life. He would leave her to live with her daughter under the care of that useless, stupid youth. He would send her whatever money he was able to send to help her get by as he had done during his father's life.

In those days, mothers were not used to opposing their sons. They were used to obeying them and responding to their wishes. The young man was now replacing his father, for he was the head of the family, the one entrusted with issuing directives and prohibitions. He should not meet with any resistance or opposition.

So it was natural that Hanena obeyed her son. And it was natural that she strove to induce Safaa to obey. Safaa does not need to be forced to obey. For she is by nature obedient to her brother's wishes and her mother's preferences. Since when have young girls been able to contradict their brothers' and mothers' orders? Her will obeys but her heart rebels. Hanena tries earnestly to entice her daughter with the temptations her son has described to her: prosperity and comfort, elevation of position and distinction of class, and opportunities to enjoy such trappings and luxuries as would not be available to her if she were to marry that modest, poor young man who, after exertion and toil—and even with the supplement of his mother's help in securing the family's needs—earns barely enough to eat.

Safaa would listen to these speeches and she would obey by will while remaining rebellious of heart, attempting to feign contentment but failing to find the means to do so.

The news of the engagement travels from Hanena's home to Morgana's, then to other homes. It becomes the talk of the people in the streets, then the talk of those who know the family. Morgana hears, and says nothing. Mu'allim Yunan hears, smiles, and says only, "And what is our son compared to this young man? Our son is a clerk who barely earns his livelihood, and this young man is a distinguished employee."

As for the people, some rejoice for Safaa but most envy her. 'Abd al-Sayyid is completely outraged. Once he threatens to commit a wicked deed, and once to commit suicide, then he subsides into a furtive calm that conceals a great evil. He comes and goes between his parents and his work, engrossed in himself, his soul twisted with what it carries. He speaks to no one of the engagement and the anticipated marriage, nor does he like to hear of them. If the people speak to him of these matters, he avoids the subject and pays it no heed, as though he were a stranger and cared nought for what the people around him do or say.

Morgana had braced herself to shower her son with sympathy and tenderness to give him solace in his afflic- tion and comfort him in this calamity that had befallen him, rendered life hateful to him, and dropped a dense screen between him and hope. But she perceived no sadness in her son and heard no lamentations. She strove to penetrate his very soul, but got nowhere. In the end she concluded that she had made too much of a small matter and overes- timated her son, presuming that he was in love and was happy with love and that this engagement had thrown him into a state of unbearable depression, grief, and despair. She scrutinizes her son and finds him merely distracted and absent-minded, caring about no one and nothing, re- vealing nothing that suggests he is aggrieved or desperate or melancholic. So she concludes the young man had been frivolous in his love and was unruffled now that the ties between him and this love had been severed—he is merely waiting for a new opportunity to have another frivolous relationship with another girl.

Undoubtedly Morgana was not pleased with her son's absent-mindedness and alienation. It must have secretly hurt her and added a new sadness to her original sorrow. It must have added to her original, now familiar, disap- pointment in him over his failure to do as well in his work as his father had done, and to earn as much money as his father had earned. It must have added a new disappoint- ment, this inability to love well and to despair when cut off from that love and separated from the one he loves. She readdresses her sympathy and tenderness, her compassion and pity, to her wretched, dejected self, which had hoped to find some relief in expressing such sympathy, tenderness, compassion, and pity as nestle in mothers' hearts.

I do not know which hurt Morgana more cruelly: her renewed disappointment in her only son, or being obliged to suppress her emotions and revert to barrenness after being on the verge of fertility, and to poverty after being on the doorstep of fortune, and to death after beginning to live.

Nothing moves a mother's spirit to agonizing despair more than this deprivation to which she is sometimes violently thrown back. For what is a mother's spirit if she is unable to express sympathy for her son and compassion for him when he hurts or is exposed to pain? And what is a mother's spirit if she cannot experience satisfaction, joy, and admiration when her son brings forth that which calls for satisfaction, joy, and admiration?

Here is Morgana, robbed of savoring satisfaction in her son and admiration of him for so long. She sees her neighbor Hanena, completely satisfied with her son Nasif and totally admiring of him, her satisfaction and admiration enhanced by the respect and praise the people around her bear for him. They do not call her by her maiden name as they did in the past, nor by 'Umm Nasif' (Mother of Nasif) as they had done after her son was born or when he was a child or an adolescent attending school or when he was an absent employee, invisible to their eyes, and their souls could not perceive the grace and elegance, beauty of dress, and awesomeness of appearance distinguishing him. They call her Umm al-Afandi ('Afandi' was the respectful title given in those days to those who had completed preparatory school), but pronounce the name as though it were all one word.

Morgana was robbed of savoring satisfaction in her son and admiration for him since she observed that he was lazy and lethargic and did not enjoy his father's qualities. Now she is robbed of what remains to her: to enfold him in her sympathy and tenderness when he is exposed to adversity, hounded by dejection, or fallen prey to depression or mis- fortune. For her son is not sensitive to adversity and dejec- tion and feels no need for sympathy or tenderness. If his mother were to embrace him with these emotions he would neither feel nor relish nor heed it. So she is unhappy in her disappointment, and unhappy in the suppression of emo- tions. She tries to talk to her old husband of this, but hears only this answer, which he gives with a sad, cynical smile: "And what is our lethargic, wretched, and desperate son compared to that impressive, handsome youth on whom life smiles!"

And Morgana attempts to speak of this one day to her son. Laughing, he says, "What have we to do with that? Money enjoys greater strength and power and influence and allure than love. Poor people should not love."

She started to continue, but he interrupted her with a long laugh, then by talking about the field and its laborers and about the estate and its employees, until his father the old man said, "Let him be. He was not created to feel ei- ther joy or sorrow, as he was not created for earnestness or work."

The youth heard his father's words and started to laugh more intensely. Then he left the house like a madman.

Behind this madness there crouched an idea that he held deep within himself—that money is more powerful than love. But the path between him and love was very short and smoothly paved. For between him and Safaa there stood only one wall. If he were to climb to the roof of the house there would be neither a wall nor a curtain nor any barrier between them. The barriers between him and en- gagement and the barriers between him and marriage were dense and forbidding. There was no means of charging or penetrating them. Since when have the poor and destitute been able to penetrate the barriers of money and wealth! Nevertheless, the barriers between him and love did not exist. All that was needed was a resourceful trick at first, followed by some audacity, and finally endurance by the soul of that which it hates.

This idea keeps imposing itself on the young man's thoughts in his waking hours, and insinuating itself into his dreams when he sleeps. He controls himself and holds his tongue. He reveals nothing and says nothing. He does not confide to others what he has concealed in his thoughts.

Safaa was in no better condition than he, but she was closer to honesty, and quicker to obey. Hers was not a difficult or complicated personality. She enjoyed neither craftiness nor cunning, but was naive and incapable of spite or intrigue. She therefore did not turn into herself or hide her inner thoughts. Rather she acquiesced, as I said, with obedient will and a rebellious heart.

When the insistence intensified and temptations increased around her, when various delicacies and presents began to cascade into the house, half her self was gratified, half wrathful. To the engagement and marriage she ceded an outward smile and a satisfaction that would occasionally radiate on her face. And to love she ceded a private grief and a buried hope, and tears that perhaps fell when she was left to herself at some time of day or night.

She had not yet seen her fiancé or heard him speak, but had seen his traces and heard reports of him.

Her fiancé was a shadow who sent delicacies, presents, and adornments, and of whom people said what they wished. Her loved one was a person she had seen close up and had listened to and spoken to. She imagined him in her soul, and conjured him in her thoughts. For some time now she saw him only in stealth. But she saw him anyway. She could, if she so desired, find the means by which to meet him, and if she did so she could resume talking to him and listening to him, and she could please him with such words and such glances as used to please him, and she could delight in those words and those glances that used to delight her.

Notions begin to occur to the girl. They are closely similar to the notions that occur to her loved one. Perhaps it occurred to Safaa that, had her neighbor been affluent and enjoyed ample income, no one would have been able to keep her away from him or to prevent her from loving him. But he is lethargic and earns only enough to keep him and his parents alive. How can poverty be added to poverty, wretchedness to wretchedness, destitution to destitution? Is it true then that love was not created for the poor, and that the poor were not created to love, but were made to toil and drudge and labor and earn their living, so that if they accomplished in this what they desired, then good for them, and if they failed to accomplish it, then there was room to accommodate them in wretchedness, and death would be a comfort and relief?

Thus did the girl's soul sway with that same pain, sorrow, and despair that swayed the young man's soul. Her heart knew the same anguish and despair that filled his heart. She would have liked nothing more than to confide her innermost feelings to him. And he would have liked nothing more than to confide his innermost feelings to her. There was no means of achieving this within people's sight or even away from it, for they were prohibited from meeting. Yet only one thin wall separated them, and were each of them to stealthily climb up to the roof, they would be able to meet and talk.

The days nevertheless go by, followed by the nights. Mu'allim Yunan's confinement to his stone bench increases. Morgana's wanderings with her tray covered in grass also increase. The boy continues with his lazy working life and his inert, dazed waking hours.

Activity picks up and commotion intensifies in Safaa's home. People sense that the wedding is slowly becoming more and more imminent.

The day finally arrived and was received by Safaa with a smile on her lips and misery in her soul. She feigned pleasure and concealed wrath. In the evening, the priests came to the home of cheerful joy teeming with cheerful, joyful people. They performed their rites: they recited the liturgy, placed the wedding crowns, rang the bells and triangles, and tied the knot that is severed only by death.

Mu'allim Yunan was lying on his bench to the right of his house and Morgana, morose and brooding, sat not very far from him. Silent tears flowed down her face. Mu'allim Yunan said, "Where is your son, Morgana?"

She answered in a depressed voice, "Did you expect him to attend this wedding?"

The old man then falls back to his silence and the old woman falls back to her morose weeping.

That day no fire was lit in Morgana's home and it saw no light that night. But the fire was burning bright and the light was radiant in Hanena's home. Half the night is gone, then two thirds, and the guests are still at their joy and jubilation. They have started to look forward to such evidence of a bride's maidenhood as was presented on such nights. But they leave without seeing, or hearing, anything. They are filled with an icy coldness. The defeated night witnesses a young man creeping out of Hanena's home, seeking anonymity in the remnants of darkness. The morning dawns, pale and cheerless. The sun shines with God's light, but through its radiance it sends forth tepid, spiritless, depleted rays that barely manage to pull the morning from its stillness and deliver it to motion, and barely manage to pull the people from their silence and deliver them to speech.

And here are some people coming along the canal bank until they reach the slope where they descend to Morgana's home, carrying a body into it. The train had completely severed its head. Morgana's voice rises in wails. Before it travels beyond her home, it is met by another wailing voice, raised with lamentations, from Hanena's home. And the people learn, before the morning is half done, that the young man had lain down awaiting death until the train from Upper Egypt brought it to him, and that Safaa is now a married woman with the standing of a divorcee, and that the knot tied by the priests, which only death can sever, has been severed.

Hanena says through her weeping, "Would that we had not come into contact with money."

And Morgana says through her weeping, "Would that we had not come into contact with love."

And Mu'allim Yunan says in his calm, creaky voice, "We have come into contact with death, which is more powerful than money and love together."

Danger

There is nothing I detest as intensely as sermonizing and preaching, warning the inattentive, awakening the sleeping, or cautioning those on whom neither caution nor forewarning has any effect. Yet, I am absolutely compelled to do so. I feel it is a duty that true patriotism and human dignity impose. It is forced on me by my concern that Egypt should not be exposed to untimely and violent dangers, and by my dream that my wretched homeland should follow its path slowly, gently, and calmly, without being hit by storms or exposed to such uneventful revolutions as have occurred in some nations.

The reader may panic upon reading these words. I truly hope that his panic should be sincere and should penetrate his heart and the depths of his conscience and propel him into action that will guard Egypt from the terrors that await it on its road to development and advancement.

Let us take, for example, a state official—not an employee whose wages are calculated on a daily basis but a permanently appointed official, as the government people say. This official has reached the seventh grade. His salary amounts to twelve pounds or a little less. He has a wife and five children. Circumstances have deemed it his fate that he should support his sisters' six children and an aunt who can no longer earn her own living. They are therefore fourteen persons living, or expected to live, on this meager salary. Living consists of food, drink, and clothing. It consists of finding refuge in a house with a roof to shelter them and walls to protect them from being taken away by the police, as the homeless are taken away. Naturally, this meager salary fails to meet the needs of such a huge family.

So borrowing ensues, then the inability to pay the debt, then the refusal of creditors to loan, since they do not retrieve their loans. Then comes privation, not from the luxuries of life—for such a family has no hope of obtaining luxuries—but privation from what sustains life and wards off the pain of hunger. Then follows privation, not from the clothes that protect against the heat of summer and the cold of winter—for such a family has no hope of obtaining such clothes—but privation from clothing to conceal those parts of the body that should be concealed. Then follows privation not from soft beds—for such a family has no hope of obtaining soft beds—but from the straw mats that lie between their bodies and the ground and from such covers as they imagine they are using to ward off the cold. Then follows weariness with life, then turning to the rich in an appeal for aid, then the turning away of the rich from those wretched petitioners, because the hearts of the rich are cruel; or because these petitioners are not the only seekers of help, but have rivals in the seeking of charity; or because the rich feel that although it is their duty to deal out alms, this should be organized so that it does not spread, and in such a way as to prevent both the wretched and the pretenders of wretchedness from resorting to them, and to prevent begging from becoming a trade and a skill and the giving of alms from being adopted as an instrument for whetting people's greed for the ease of the affluent that is beyond their grasp; or because of all these reasons and of many others that may be added to them, the counting of which is of no use to any one.

What is not in doubt is that this state official is unable to find in his paltry salary enough to satisfy his family's minimal requirements for survival. He borrows from one source or another until he can no longer borrow. Then he seeks charity from every direction, but cannot obtain it. There remains no resort for him other than to commit sin to enable him and his family to live. His conscience and his religion might keep him from committing a sin, or the need for food and clothing may be more persuasive. But the law lies in wait for him if he does stray, and he is exposed to punishment and his family to misery redoubled by these new circumstances.

Then let him be patient. Yet patience does not feed the hungry, nor clothe the naked, nor still the child who screams for food when he is bitten by hunger, nor heal the sick, nor relieve the pains of those who have fallen to the lowermost level of privation.

There is no doubt that this official is not alone in this appalling destitution, nor is he the sole bearer of this heavy burden. There are others like him, counted not in tens or hundreds, but in thousands and, I fear, in tens of thousands. It is not possible that the problems of these people could be solved by borrowing and by the inability to pay debts or by the avoidance of debts. It is not possible that the problems of these people could be solved by benevolence and charity. Benevolence and charity may serve to relieve passing crises, or to feed the children for a few days or clothe them for a season. But they cannot provide these people with a life in which they are insured against wretchedness and hunger.

I have not, until now, even mentioned the rights of the children to an education and to a state of health that guards them against fatal plagues or contagious diseases and that precludes their becoming a source of danger to the people who come in contact with them.

If this problem were a transient one, I would have felt that talking about it would draw attention to it and generate discussion and attempts to resolve it. But it did not arise today or yesterday. It has been with us for a long time and we have continuously neglected it. For this reason it is producing its outrageous and scandalous results: the easy spreading of the plague; corruption, bribery, and theft; the alienation of people from one another; the spread of darkness in people's consciences and hearts; the spread of despair, even in God's relief; the spread of abasement and affected humility and disgrace; and the spread of submission to injustice, capitulation to tyranny, and compliance with the oppression of freedom and dignity, in contempt of all that makes us human let alone all that makes us distinguished and civilized. All these diseases and disgraces have but one source: wretchedness.

Let us return to the state official. Like other officials, he goes to his office in the morning and returns to his home in the evening. He wears clothes that suit his position. If his clothes become worn out, and he is unable to find the means to purchase new ones, he will be penalized. For the state is keen that its employees should be noble in appearance at least. He therefore comes and goes in those suitable clothes of his, with a tarboush on his head, and shoes on his feet that must never wear out.

He receives the people who seek his services, smiling or frowning in their faces, serving them contentedly or reluctantly. He converses with his colleagues, joking with them at times and complaining at others. He is in all events a moving corpse, alive in appearance but dead in his heart, killed by wretchedness and misery and worry. Most of his colleagues are like him.

I wonder at a nation that is served by officials whose bodies live but whose souls have died. Should I expect, after this, that this nation should carry its people on the road to self-esteem and pride and to complete or even partial independence? What is astounding is that we have lived to see the day when state officials ask for charity and seek alms: they ask for it with their tongues and with their pens. They have strained with all their abilities until need has compelled them to cast off that dignity that God has granted to man, and which deters him from begging or seeking charity.

State officials, then, ask for alms and seek charity. What is most astounding is that the general public envies the officials their established, systematized salaries, dealt out to them on the first of the month, and which is never delayed in reaching them. If this is the condition of the envied, then how is it for the envious?

I think that by now you will have perceived the danger that is chasing us or that we are rushing toward. I think that you will now agree with me that we have two choices: either we leave matters as they are and allow the inevitable to take place, and allow what has befallen nations before to befall us, or we confront what we have created and try to reform so that we may deter state officials (and thereby all people) from asking for alms and seeking charity.

There is only one way to do so: to reconsider our whole social system, including the taxes the state collects and the wages it confers. The taxes are very small, lower than they should be, and the wages are very small, lower than they should be. Justice dictates that the taxes should be doubled, and that the wages should be doubled, and that the state should cease its draining of public funds, and that the rich should cease draining their private funds.

There is no means of realizing social reform unless the suitable political tool is made available, one that is capable of allaying society's burdens and saving it from its problems. Do you feel that Egypt possesses, these days, the suitable political tool with which to attempt such a reform? This is a question I do not need to answer.

Social Awareness

The second caliph, 'Umar ibn al-Khattab, may God have mercy on his soul, did not realize when he led the Muslims from the pilgrimage in the eighteenth year of the Hijra (A.D. 639), that he and the Muslims of Arabia, of Hijaz, of Najd, and especially of Tuhama, were embarking on a dim, dark year that would test their consciences, their wealth, and their morality. They would be tested in whatever share they had been granted of patience in the face of distress, perseverance in the face of calamity, and forbearance in the face of misfortune. They would be tested for that noble, distinguished sentiment that renders a human being truly human and promotes him to an exalted position in the ranks of chivalry.

It is that sentiment of sympathy, comradeship, and social awareness that makes each individual feel, whatever his rank, that he belongs to a group in whose happiness he finds his happiness, and in whose misery he finds misery. He is a member of a group from which he takes his share of whatever felicity and wretchedness come its way, and whatever prosperity and adversity are meted out to it.

'Umar did not realize that destiny had reserved this cruel trial for him and for the Muslims of the Arab nations in order to purify their hearts and cleanse their souls and teach them that life is not all well-being or lasting contentment, that it does not possess fertility to be renewed with every new season, but is a mixture of felicity and wretchedness, of delight and pain, of happiness and sorrow.

Destiny did so to teach them that the righteous course for the believer whose heart has been truly touched by faith is not to exceed his bounds if he becomes rich or to be ungrateful if he finds fortune, nor to despair if he is tried by wretchedness or misery. He should not covet well-being for himself if he alone is granted prosperity, nor should he leave his brethren prey to calamities and misfortunes when they occur, but should give to the people some of what he has until they share his prosperity, and take from them some of what they have until he shares their wretchedness.

For God has not spread the sun's light for one faction to enjoy alone, nor sent the breeze for one party to breathe alone, nor drawn the rivers or let flow the springs for one group of people to drink and another to thirst, nor sprouted plants from the ground to satiate one people and starve another.

Rather, God has dealt out his blessings in abundance for all people to enjoy, their share in it varying in size. But deprivation should not be imposed on any one of them, whoever he may be, whatever his class or his position among his countrymen.

'Umar did not appreciate, when he emerged from the season of pilgrimage that year, that God would send to the Muslims a new year in which He would try them with hunger, thirst, and nakedness. It would be a trial that they had not known the likes of for a very long time.

How could 'Umar have foretold this when the affairs of his growing nation were running as well as the Muslims could have wanted? It enjoyed all the justice and far-reaching fame they could desire as well as the spread of its conquests, the proliferation of security, and the abundance of prosperity.

Yet the new year arrived and the sky was niggardly with its water until the earth was scorched with thirst and as black as ashes, and until the Muslims were compelled to call this the Year of Ash. The sky was niggardly with its water and the sun gave liberally of its heat and the earth failed to produce what the people could eat or what they could feed to the bleating and frothing creatures for which they bargained.

'Umar settled in the city and beheld the crisis. It was advancing slowly, taking its time. But it was confident and pressing in its course. He witnessed the desert people growing impoverished, poverty overwhelming them until they could think of nothing but to hasten to their caliph asking for whatever would feed them in their hunger, water them in their thirst, and clothe them in their nakedness.

Why should he not do so when he had taken their sons and fathers, their brothers, their bread-winners and their supporters, and hurled them into breaches and driven them into wars, the beginning of which they knew, but the end of which they were ignorant of.

Why should they not hasten to him when they saw his love, sympathy, and affection for them. He would visit those living furthest away as well as the closest, never failing to go to them whatever the hour of the night or day.

'Umar saw that the entire Arab Peninsula was sending him its surviving elderly men, its women, its children, its disabled who were capable of nothing, and its able members who were capable but found nothing to be capable of.

Here 'Umar rises to face this violent crisis in the manner of a man who comprehends equity as no man after him has done, and who assumes a burden as no man after him has done. He rises as a man who faces calamity, determined to overcome it or to die remedying it, regardless of the consequences, until the Year of Ash becomes one of the inexhaustible and eternal treasures of Muslims, in which they can find an example, a noble moral and a righteous paradigm that no heart enjoying any share of gentleness or leniency can reject, unless it be one of those hearts that God in His glory and splendor has described as being as hard as rock or even crueler.

'Umar started with himself in resisting this calamity, re - fusing to be anything but one among the Muslims: suffering as they suffered, hungering as they hungered, thirsting as they thirsted, and straining himself and his family as much as the crisis was straining the most destitute and wretched of the people.

He did so because he believed, before anything else, that it was his duty to himself, to God, and to the people to do so. He did so also because he believed that it was his duty to teach the people how reciprocation, cooperation, and empathy should be exercised in times of trial and when calamities occur. He therefore insisted on living as the most destitute of the people lived.

He learned that the Muslims were able to obtain ghee only with great difficulty and exertion, so he resolved to deprive himself of ghee until the common people were able to obtain it. He imposed on himself a diet of oil and dry bread. When the oil became too distressing for his stom - ach, he thought that if it were cooked it would be more di - gestible, and he ordered that his food should be cooked in oil. But the cooked oil was even more painful and difficult to digest. His complexion changed from its natural light - ness and darkened.

Then he started to feed the people at public tables, join - ing them and eating what they ate.

Then he ordered the public criers to announce among the people that whoever wanted to come to these tables and eat at them might do so, and that whoever wanted to come and carry away his need of this food to eat with his family might do so. He supervised the preparation of the food himself. At times he even taught the cooks how to cook.

Yet the crisis continued to grow more and more severe. The Bedouins converged on the city, although many of them were unable to move at all—the crops had been de - stroyed, their animals' udders had dried out, and the cattle had died.

It became the caliph's duty to reach these people in their dwellings and to deliver their livelihood to them, since they were unable to seek it themselves.

Now 'Umar writes to his representatives in the provinces, ordering them to send him provisions. I read this short, wonderful letter, which 'Umar wrote to his representative in Egypt, 'Amr ibn al-'As, may God have mercy on his soul. I perceive in this short, wonderful letter a savage violence filled with great compassion and unsurpassable gentleness:

> In the name of God the Compassionate, the Merciful.
>   From the slave of God, the Prince of the Faithful,
> to the 'Asi ('disobeyer'), son of the disobeying:
> Peace be upon you. Do you behold me and my
> people being consumed while you and your people
> live? Help! Help! Help!

As soon as 'Amr ibn al-'As read this letter in which the Prince of the Faithful severely rebuked him, he wrote back:

> In the name of God the Compassionate, the Merciful.
>   To God's slave 'Umar, the Prince of the Faithful,
> from 'Amr ibn al-'As.
>   Peace be upon you. I thank God, the One and
> Only. Relief has come to you to stay and stay. I
> swear to send a string of camels of which the first
> will be where you are while the last is still here.

Then 'Amr started to send relief by sea and by land. 'Umar wrote to his other representatives in Syria and Iraq, and they all did as his representative in Egypt had done.

Then 'Umar sent his messengers to the borders of the Arab countries beyond Syria and Iraq and Egypt and ordered them to collect relief and take it to the Bedouins in their dwellings and to feed, dress, and water them. He urged these messengers not to weaken or yield and not to distribute the food they carried unless they were sure that it was destined for the stomachs of the hungry and not the stores of the hoarders.

More wonderful than all this, and an even more inspiring example, is the statement of 'Umar that: "We shall feed them with whatever we have to feed them with, and when we run short we will charge the members of the able homes with the care of their number from among the needy, until God brings forth relief."

Obviously, he opened the doors of the treasury wide and resolved to provide for the people from it. When he found no more there, he instructed each rich family to feed a number of poor people equal to the number of its members, thus employing the authority of the law and of religion, until God was to bring forth relief.

I have not related all this to amuse you with the splendors of history or to divert you with these wonderful anecdotes from the life of the Prince of the Faithful, 'Umar ibn al-Khattab. For this is not a time of amusement or distraction. We are living now in dismal days that are no less atrocious, and are perhaps even more atrocious, than the Year of Ash.

For in 'Umar's day, and in that year, the Muslims found hunger, thirst ,and nakedness. The Egyptians, this year, confront death and sickness, and after death and sickness they confront the hunger, thirst, and nakedness that the Arabs found in the Year of Ash.

It is the right of Egyptians on whom the plague has descended that it should be warded off them and that its effects should be warded off them, until there is not one among them who complains of hunger, thirst, or nakedness.

It is the duty of the state to provide this right as long as it can find in its treasury the funds that enable it to do so. It should think of nothing else until it is rid of this trial, and if its treasury does not salvage it, then it has a duty to follow the means that 'Umar followed, and to impose the care of the destitute upon the able until God brings forth relief.

The state must learn, and the rich must learn, that giving alms is a good deed in times of prosperity and ease. But when duress is extreme and the crisis intense and when a plague strikes, then giving alms is not a good deed but a duty imposed by justice. And if people do not perform this duty spontaneously, then it is the duty of the state to coerce them to do so.

The state must learn that in times of prosperity and ease God commanded the leaders of the Muslims to take from the rich and give to the poor, until no hungry or deprived person remains among the people.

Thus when matters become serious and a catastrophe occurs, it is a sin for the affluent to eat or drink or dress until the hungry have eaten and the thirsty have drunk and the naked have been clothed. And it is the state's duty to see that this is done by authority of the law. If it does not do so then it has committed the greatest of sins in its obligations toward God, toward the homeland, and toward its countrymen.

These are the lessons in social awareness that 'Umar ibn al-Khattab gave to the rulers and the ruled. They are based neither on socialism nor on communism, but on God's Holy words:

> Lo! Allah enjoineth justice and kindness, and
> giving to kinsfolk, and forbiddeth lewdness and
> abomination and wickedness. He exhorteth you in
> order that ye may take heed. (*XVI, 90*)

So can we be so bold as to hope that the nation will heed, and that the wealthy will heed? Can we be so bold as to hope that the nation will remember, and that the wealthy will remember? Can we be so bold as to ask that we be excused—and that human dignity be excused—the begging of alms through newspapers from people who place riches on the same level as country and countrymen?

It is the state's duty to instruct the close-fisted in how generosity and heeding the authority of the law should be exercised when these are not forthcoming from wakeful consciences and chaste souls.

The Burden of Wealth

'Abd al-Rahman ibn 'Uf had ample wealth. He was one of the earliest believers, who eagerly embraced Islam when the calling came. His fortune had not spoiled him nor had his wealth turned his heart away from godliness. Unlike the other prosperous members of the Quraysh tribe, he did not fear Islam's call for equality between rich and poor, between powerful and weak, between free men and slaves. Rather, God gifted him with a ready acceptance of Islam. He embraced it with a passion, sacrificing to it the money, wealth, and power he had accumulated. He was ready to endure, alongside his friends, exposure to harm and adversity.

When the trial intensified, insurrection grew arduous, and affliction grew, he did not hesitate, as his friends did not hesitate, to flee with his religion to a place where he could safely nurture his beliefs and worship his God, abandoning his extensive fortune and elevated position, abandoning his people and his family, whom he had deeply loved and on whom he had conferred the most sincere gentleness, charity, and tenderness, with which his heart brimmed.

He took part in the two flights to Ethiopia and in the flight to al-Madina, which the Prophet, God's prayers and peace be on him, adopted as the home of Islam.

He arrived there possessing only his noble heart, pure conscience, staunch pride, and faith that filled his soul with confidence and conviction.

The Prophet, God's prayers and peace be on him, had introduced him to a wealthy member of the Ansar (the Madinans who embraced Islam), Sa'd ibn al-Rabi'i al-Khazarji, God grant him peace. Sa'd told him, "Behold my money and take half. I have two wives. I will divorce whichever one of them is more pleasing to you, and you may have her as your wife."

'Abd al-Rahman answered, "God Bless you. When I wake up in the morning direct me to your marketplace."

When he awoke he went to the market, where he spent the bulk of the day. When he returned he had bought and sold, and earned his means of living. A while later he joined the Prophet's council, attired in new clothes and be-decked with such ornaments as were permitted the Muslims in those days. When the Prophet inquired about his appearance, he told him that he had taken a woman of the city as his wife and that he had given her a dowry in gold. The Prophet then ordered him to join his friends, and he did so.

Within a few years, 'Abd al-Rahman ibn 'Uf had become one of al-Madina's wealthy men, having acquired a fortune to replace another and accumulated money to replace money. He had managed to marry and to offer a dowry of thirty thousand dirhams. He would say, "I felt myself unable to lift even a stone without suspecting that I would find gold or silver beneath it."

'Abd al-Rahman was therefore one of the very rich even before Mecca was won over to Islam, and when it was conquered he added his new wealth to his old.

Then he invested all this in the best manner, adopting the methods followed by Quraysh, until one day he became one of the richest of all Arabs and perhaps even the richest except for the third caliph, 'Usman ibn 'Affan, may God have mercy on his soul. It could even be claimed that 'Abd al-Rahman ibn 'Uf was wealthier than the Muslim treasury in the day of the Prophet, God's prayers and peace be on him.

For in those times the treasury did not save anything and taxes were not collected for it, nor was anything worth mention placed in it. Easy booty was made from raids and divided among the raiders, save for a fifth that was set aside for public utilities and for charity and benevolence. Alms were collected from the rich and distributed among the poor, while only a minimum sum reached the city. When it did, it was set aside for those expenses designated by God in the Holy Quran.

The treasury was therefore poor. Nothing is more indicative of this than the Prophet's persistent urging of the rich to support his raids with their money, either by handing over some of their surplus or relinquishing some of their assets.

The Prophet hated nothing so much as he hated the accumulation of money. He dreaded, for himself and for his companions, nothing so much as the accumulation of money and the spread of wealth.

One day he looked at 'Abd al-Rahman and said to him, "Ibn 'Uf, you are one of the wealthy, and you will only enter heaven crawling. Lend to God and He will liberate your legs."

'Abd al-Rahman ibn 'Uf said, "How much should I lend to God, O Prophet of God?"

Said the Prophet, "Start with what you had as of last evening."

Said Ibn 'Uf, "All of it, O Prophet?"

"Yes."

Ibn 'Uf left with this intention. The Prophet later sent him a message saying the angel Gabriel had instructed him to "command Ibn 'Uf to host the guests and feed the poor and give to the needy, starting with those whom he supports. If he does so it will be sufficient tithes for his condition."

*

Before proceeding, I invite the reader to pause with me and to perceive the splendid naiveté or naive splendor of the wording, the meaning, and the story of the above conversation.

The Prophet is anxious for 'Abd al-Rahman because of his great wealth, seeing this fortune as a ponderous and oppressive burden on his shoulders, preventing him from walking, constraining his movement as though he were bound and unable to walk to heaven on his feet alongside the other marchers, or to run to it with the runners. He does not instruct him to relieve himself of his burden by totally discarding it. Rather, he instructs him to invest it rather than waste it by offering God a guaranteed loan. His money is not lost, but will be reimbursed to him on the Day of Judgment greatly multiplied.

'Abd al-Rahman inquires as to the share of money he has to lend God, and is told, "Start with what you had when you faced the evening."

In other words: rise and distribute as tithes all the money you had accumulated when you began the evening. Know that when you do so you are only beginning and that you will be tested in the money you accumulate in your future days as you have been tested in the money you have accumulated in your past days.

The test was a little severe for 'Abd al-Rahman. He asks the Prophet, "With all the money that I have accumulated?"

The Prophet answers, "Yes."

'Abd al-Rahman rises and resolves to execute the commands of God and His Prophet concerning the money he loves and in the accumulation and investment of which he has exhausted time and effort, and borne hardship and strain. There is no harm in his loving money. But it is a serious fault, and a supreme offense, that the love of money should prevent him from spending it on charity for orphans and the poor.

Has God not described Godliness to the Muslims not as having to face the east or the west in prayer but as faith in God and the offering of money, despite one's love of it, to those who need it?

'Abd al-Rahman then rises, determined to deal with his money as God and the Prophet have commanded him. But then the Prophet sends him word that God and His Prophet have taken pity on him and command him to take in guests, feed the poor, and give to those who ask, starting with his family and his children. If he does so then he will have totally sanctified his soul and completely purified his money.

Thus it was a test of steadfastness under trial, until sincere determination on obedience, however difficult, and sacrifice, however precious, and endeavor, however laborious, are proven. When this steadfast determination and these sincere motives were discerned, then God and his Prophet alleviated some of the weight of the burdens.

God called His Prophet to His side, and direct communication with the Heavens were severed and the Muslims were denied the revelations that used to accompany them in their mornings and nights.

Then one morning the people awoke to a violent commotion that echoed throughout the city. 'A'isha, the wife of the Prophet, mother of the faithful, may God grant her peace, asks about it, and is told: these are the camels of 'Abd al-Rahman ibn 'Uf. She said, "I heard the Prophet, God's prayers and peace be on him, saying, 'It is as though I see 'Abd al-Rahman ibn 'Uf walking on the righteous road, now deviating from it, now proceeding in a straight line, until he is almost on the verge of slipping.'"

'A'isha's words reached 'Abd al-Rahman. The caravan numbered five hundred camels carrying precious goods from Syria. When he heard these words he said, "These camels and what they carry are alms!"

He was not satisfied to give away part of what the camels bore, or to give away the camels without their burden, but gave away both the camels and what they bore.

Had the Prophet lived longer, and had the revelations continued and the words of Heaven continued to descend to earth, perhaps the Prophet would have accepted that 'Abd al-Rahman should offer only some of his trade as alms, and allowed him to keep the remainder. But 'A'isha had only repeated what she had heard from the Prophet of God.

On hearing her words, 'Abd al-Rahman feared that he would now deviate from the righteous road, now proceed on a straight line, only reaching heaven with much effort. He was keen to proceed in a straight line on the righteous road, avoiding any deviation or confusion, until he reached heaven without slipping, and without exertion or drudgery.

'Abd al-Rahman was one of the most charitable and generous of all the Muslims. He was one of the most faithful and compassionate toward people. He spent his whole life investing his money through paying tithes. Yet this did not decrease his wealth. Rather, it increased and compounded it. It was as though God had resolved that He would reward him for his charity, and reimburse his loan in multiples, not only in the other world but also in this.

This is an old story. But the days in which we live give it a new life. I recount it to those who have been allowed the wealth and fortune 'Abd al-Rahman was allowed, or even more.

I want this to sink into their hearts: that if wealth weighed heavily on 'Abd al-Rahman—despite the fact that he was one of the first believers, that he had sacrificed himself and his money in support of the Prophet, and that not a day of his life passed without his distributing much in alms, and despite the fact that the Prophet had guaranteed him and all the other first believers entrance into heaven—then it should weigh upon them even more heavily. For they are not among the first to embrace Islam, they did not sacrifice themselves and their money in the name of God, and the Prophet guaranteed them nothing save that if they obeyed God's commandments concerning themselves and their money, then nothing they offered would be lost to them.

If the Prophet worried that 'Abd al-Rahman would only reach heaven crawling, and that he would follow the righteous road only with effort, then we have more reason to worry that our rich will be unable to reach heaven even crawling and will be unable to follow the righteous road with or without effort.

May our rich recognize the wretchedness, misery, plague, and death that surround them.

May they recognize the fact that their money is a simple, returnable loan and that those who lend to God righteously will have their loan refunded in multiples on the Day of Judgment, while those who hoard gold and silver and do not spend it in the name of God have been promised excruciating torment on the day the fires of hell become fierce and burn their brows, sides, and backs, the day when they will be told

> Here is that which ye hoarded for yourselves.
> Now taste of what ye used to hoard. (*IX, 35*)

Generosity

I do not know if these tales are factual, as I would like them to be and as I think they are, or if they are fictitious, as the detractors would like them to be and think they are. Whether they be true or not, they rouse many notions in my mind and stir many emotions in my heart, and drive me to much thought, as they drive me to dream many beautiful dreams that, if realized, would represent the attainment of the greatest hope, and that, if not realized, would still have allowed me to live a few happy hours, as the old poet used to say.

These are tales about the generosity of the generous, the benevolence of the benevolent, and the contribution by the rich of part of the wealth they are granted and the riches they are sent. Thanks be to God who has not created all people covetous of money, miserly with what they possess, obtaining a measure of wealth only to wish for a greater measure, and realizing a share of fortune only to ask for further fortune. And yet, with the abundance of what they own, the abundance of what they obtain, and the abundance of the riches they accumulate, they are most like a deep, bottomless rock. For such a rock allows not a drop of the water that settles into it to seep out, however much it increases and accumulates. It is solid on all sides, providing for anyone roving around it and wanting its contents no option other than to shatter it utterly.

Thanks be to God who has not created all people as covetous and as miserly as that. He has created among them, from time to time, he who respects wealth but nevertheless does not adore it or kill himself for it or adopt it as an end in itself, but considers it a means by which to benefit himself and his family, his relatives and loved ones, up to the greatest possible number of people, whenever he is able.

These magnanimous people are a consolation for the coveting misers. They instill within you the thought that humanity is not all evil and that although peoples' lives may be a desolate and barren desert, it is not without an oasis where they may stay once in a while, one that offers the weary and exhausted traveler such shade, water, rest, and relief as allow him to forget some of the hardship he has endured, and help him to endure the hardship he is yet to encounter upon resuming his journey across his barren and desolate desert. Were it not for these magnanimous people, humanity would deserve our most intense, our most ugly, our most disdainful abhorrence.

People seek repose wherever, and however, they may find it. They therefore seek consolation wherever and however they may find it. They seek it around them, and if they cannot reach it, they wander farther away and seek it beyond distant frontiers and in remote regions. If they fail to find it in their contemporaries, they seek it in days gone by and preceding ages.

The reader may think that I am exaggerating. But I have no interest in exaggeration. I have witnessed these incidents taking place, these misfortunes occurring, and this wretchedness taking hold of the majority of Egyptians everywhere, attacking them from all directions, preparing them for death until some of them surrender to it and keeping those who survive to itself, continuing to prepare them for death, sometimes taking its time, sometimes striking swiftly.

And I have observed the wealthy people around me, and recognized their attitude toward this growing misery, dreadful terror, and profound agony. I have discerned only greed and miserliness, cruelty of hearts, coarseness of souls, harshness of temperament, and disturbance of minds.

I found people who spent while hating to spend, and others who wavered between generosity and meanness before opting for miserliness but only after great hesitation and endless thought. I found yet others who do not spend, hesitate, or think but ignore the people around them and ignore the misery, hardship, strife, and death around them. They put their fingers in their ears so as not to hear, and cover their eyes so as not to see, and bolt their hearts so as to keep out whatever might arouse feelings of solidarity, empathy, or compassion within them.

They take to their pleasures, interests, and aspirations as they perceive them, caring not a whit that they are enjoying themselves while the people around them are suffering. It does not offend them that they should luxuriate while those around them are gulping great mouthfuls of wretchedness, misery, and suffering. They dance over the bodies of their countrymen and rejoice in their wretchedness. They do not differentiate between the detestable music coming from the wails of the weeping, the moans of the ailing, and the rattling of the dying, and the music reaching them from the tunes played by musicians, the blowing of the trumpet blowers, and the dancing of the dancers. It does not disturb them when they drink from their clear, brimming cups that the essence of this liquid is the copious tears that they can neither see nor feel because they flow, not from the people's eyes, but from the eyes of the whole of Egypt.

The tears of people may be seen and felt, and may thus disturb those who see and feel them. But the tears of entire nations, of entire generations, are seen and felt only by those who have been gifted with some delicacy of heart, lucidity of spirit, purity of conscience, and sophistication of temperament. These, unfortunately, are few—nay, fewer than a few.

I faced all this and looked at the people around me to observe how they are gentle and kind to one another and how the prosperous hurry to succor the strained. Yet I saw nothing of much consequence. I observed only a little generosity and much chatter. I saw a contest in false boasting, and with all this a scurrying toward indulging in worthless delights and insipid pleasures.

I have not yet learned that the wealthy among us, with all their riches, and all the profits they make from those riches, have managed to collect a hundred thousand pounds in aid of those afflicted by the cholera. I think they are still very far from reaching this sum and doubt they will ever reach it or even come close to it.

They have started to forget the plague, after being reassured that it will not attack them—if it is possible for people to be reassured—and after the Ministry of Health has claimed that it is receding.

None of them told himself—and none wants to tell himself—that the plague has snatched away the supporters of many families and reduced these families to a state of destitution that is impossible to imagine, let alone describe. None of them has told himself—and none wants to tell himself—that these families are entitled firstly to live, secondly to find some consolation in the sympathy of their countrymen for the misfortunes that have befallen them, and thirdly to feel that they are dignified families belonging to a dignified nation.

None of this has occurred to any of them—and none wants any of it to occur to them. For they are too preoccupied with the accumulation of money upon money, the compounding of wealth upon wealth, and the indulgence in forms of pleasure and delight that they are hardly done with before moving on to further forms, and from which they are hardly rested before resuming their reveling and luxuriating.

Finally, it has not occurred to any of them—and none wants it to occur to him—that the wretchedness of the wretched and the destitution of the destitute does not reflect shame on them so much as it does on their entire nation, and on those who have been designated by circumstance as the representatives of this nation. They meet with foreigners when they visit Egypt, and seek them abroad when they do not, listening, willingly or unwillingly, to their comments on the plague and its victims, yet experiencing neither personal shame nor shame for their homeland or for this generation of Egyptians, who are branded in foreign eyes as the embodiment of detestable selfishness. This debases them and makes them worthy of being scorned and despised, honored only by those who exploit them as a means of realizing their own interests.

What harm does it do me if I witness all this and grow weary of it all? I find myself in a dilemma: either I grow to detest life and the living, rejecting country and countrymen, or I seek consolation wherever and however I may find it. Perhaps the tragedy will subside and I may find myself able, sooner or later, to return to this generation of contemporary Egyptians, especially the wealthy, and talk and listen to them without experiencing in my heart this unbearable pain and horrible revulsion.

To history then, and to the tales of the ancients. For our contemporaries have overwhelmed our hearts with despair and our spirits with despondency. Let us abandon them and travel in time, since we cannot travel in space.

Let us turn to the reports on those ancient ages, be they factual or not. If they are factual, then they are our consolation. And if they are fictitious, then they will allow us to dream of a generation of people where man is not a slave to money and subjugated to fortune, but where money is enslaved by its owner and where fortune is a means of aiding the afflicted, helping the grieving, and saving the dispossessed. And if these tales are fictitious they will be the means of arousing that sweet emotion experienced by the noble man when he feels he has aided an afflicted person, comforted a grieving person, saved one who was dispossessed, shown benevolence to a friend, or used his money rather than allowing it to use him.

To history, then. Let us forget the age in which we live. To the tales of the ancients. Let us divert ourselves from the behavior of our contemporaries.

You may believe or disbelieve me. I care nothing for that. But remember that I paused for a long time before some of these tales, narrated to us about the generous and munificent ancients. I have paused at this tale told of 'Usman ibn 'Affan when, in the days of the first caliph, Abu Bakr, the people of al-Madina became impoverished until prices rose and the poor and the middle classes were unable to secure food.

At that time 'Usman's camels arrived bearing many provisions from Syria. The tradesmen rushed to him, wanting to buy his stock and sell it to the people. He bartered with them until they offered him its price fourfold. But he refused to sell unless they paid him ten times the price. When they refused, he told them that God had promised him ten times its worth if he were to contribute it to charity. He then told them that he preferred this transaction to theirs and that he preferred God's reward to their money, and declared his provisions were to be alms for the Muslims.

Yes! And I have paused for a long time before another one of the Prophet's companions, Tulha ibn 'Abd Allah, God grant him peace. His wife came to him and found him distressed and aggrieved. When she asked him gently for the cause, he told her that he had received a large sum of money and that he was anxious, not knowing what to do with it.

Smiling, his wife responded briefly, "Share it out."

And he agreed.

He distributed the money among his relatives and friends and needy Muslims, and retired to a happy night. That money amounted to four hundred thousand dirhams.

Yes! And I pause for a long time before this Tulha still, when he sold a piece of land for seven hundred thousand dirhams. When he received the money at his home, he deliberated briefly, then said, "A man who goes to sleep possessing such money yet not knowing what God has in store for him is a vain man."

Then he ordered that the money be distributed among his relatives, friends, and needy Muslims. He did not go to sleep until he had given it all away.

The marvel is that all this distribution of wealth, despite its abundance and frequency, did not reduce Tulha to poverty or to anything close, because God has promised the rich that if they give for charity sincerely and unhypocritically, seeking no fame and attempting no falseness or duplicity, they will be reimbursed. He was killed on the Day of the Camel, and his fortune was exposed to many vagaries after his death. His heirs nevertheless inherited three million dirhams.

Would that our rich might contemplate spending the surplus of their money sincerely, without hypocrisy or deceit. For this expense would cause them no great misfortune. Would that our rich might believe God's promise or attempt to test it. Would that they might spend, sincerely and without hypocrisy, so that they may judge if God will reimburse them. But Alas! There is no hope of that.

For our rich do not read, and if they read they do not believe, and if they believe they do not dare. They find it easier to gamble with thousands in a gambling club or at a race track than to risk thousands in a benevolent cause to see whether God will fulfill his promise.

What vexes the heart and exasperates the soul is that the government sees all these manifestations of the greed and miserliness of the wealthy yet does not allow itself to impose taxes to enable it to aid the afflicted, comfort the grieving, or save the dispossessed.

For if God wishes ill on a people, then there is no evading it.

Believe me, it is completely beneficial for the wise man, the intellectual, to escape with all his heart, all his mind, and all his conscience from this generation. If he is unable to escape to another country, he can at least escape to another age in history.

Ailing Egypt

Hardly had I climbed on board the ship and settled down, being done with those infuriating procedures that are forced upon anyone setting sail, whatever port he sails from, than I learned that Egypt was ailing. I listened to this news without much attention or thought. For the item was published in a French newspaper, issued in Marseilles. Much of this type of news about Egypt is published. It neither represents the truth nor indicates anything other than the attitude of its dispatchers: hatred for Egypt, or an inclination to conspire against it and find fault with it or exaggerate whatever bad news might be reported.

In the past few months French newspapers have shown little sympathy for Egypt. They are greatly vexed by it, quick to report whatever might upset Egyptians, jumping at any opportunities that present themselves and fabricating them if they do not.

For episodes have taken place between us and France that have caused us to become reserved toward the French and made us disappointed in them, and which have caused the French to become reserved toward us and made them disappointed in us. An astute reader would be wise to be careful and reflective when he reads news of Egypt in France or news of France in Egypt.

I will not conceal from the reader that as soon as I heard the report that Egypt was ailing, that its ailment was probably cholera, and that the Egyptian government was preparing to combat the plague, I shrugged and shook my head and smiled cynically at those journalists who so clumsily wished to find fault with Egypt and to lie about it.

Day after day passed, the ship voyaging toward its desti-nation, the sea being sometimes rough with it and some-times gentle. No one mentioned the minor item of news published in an untrustworthy newspaper, through which the readers had quickly glanced.

But one evening an announcement was posted advising the passengers that potable water would be cut off for a few hours each day in order to enable the ship to reach Beirut without needing to take on water in Egypt, since it was afflicted with cholera.

Now we did not shrug or shake our heads or smile cyni-cally or gravely. Instead the passengers gazed at one an-other in silence, then gathered together and discussed the matter in bewilderment. As for me, I admit that I too did not shrug or shake my head, but bowed it to the ground and began to grow smaller and smaller, wishing that I could become invisible to the people around me and that I would not have to answer if they spoke to me.

For the sentiment that seized me at that moment was not one of fear, or of the need to take precaution. It was a strange sentiment, which, I now realize, was a mixture of sorrow and shame.

I felt sorrow for the homeland that we felt deserved happiness. We had sacrificed our youth and our old age, our efforts and our strength, in our attempt to deliver it some of that happiness. Yet here we are, helpless wit-nesses to the misery flooding it, the plague overtaking it in all parts, and pain and catastrophe rushing at it from every direction. We see miserable wretchedness drowning the great majority of its people, clinging to them with a grip that never relaxes. They are hungry, naked, and ignorant. They are unhappy for all this. Many of them are even more unhappy because they are aware of their misery and are aware of their right to be happy. Many of them long to be rid of their misery and to attain some measure of happiness. Yet they are unable to realize their aspirations. They do not know how to realize them, and find no one to help them do so.

I felt sorrow for the homeland that we felt deserved freedom and security, and for which we had sacrificed our youth and old age, our efforts and our strength, in our attempt to win some of its rightful freedom and security. Yet here we are, helpless, watching it chained and unable to move, tongue-tied and unable to speak, with its heart benumbed and unable to enjoy the sentiments other free peoples enjoy, even the most elementary human pride. We behold and find it afraid and cautious because of all this: afraid to act lest it anger its masters, afraid to speak lest it offend them, and afraid to remain silent lest it further demean itself in its oppressors' eyes. It vacillates between action and inertia, between outcry and silence, between sentiment and frigidity.

And then I felt sorrow for the homeland that we felt deserved independence, and for which we sacrificed our youth and our old age, our efforts and our strength, to earn this independence. Yet we behold and witness it being refused its rights most violently and cruelly. And the victors, who only yesterday were ingratiating themselves to it and flattering it, are now consorted against it, disavowing and conspiring against it, all of which represents nothing less than tyranny and treachery, injustice and ingratitude.

And finally I felt sorrow for the country where all schools of politics, culture, and economy originated, and to which God granted fair weather, fertile land, clear skies, and a river overflowing with grace and blessings. All this should have been enough to provide its people with a bearable material life, and to deflect diseases and plagues from it.

Yet we behold and witness that it has been deprived of such a life. We witness diseases and plagues rushing at it from the farthest east and the farthest south, finding no one to fend them off or to protect it from their evil. So diseases and plagues descend from its clear sky, sprout from its fertile land, and flow from its ample river! So its people are the grazing ground for diseases and plagues, which are free to snatch away whoever they wish, however, whenever, and wherever they wish!

So in less than a month the whole world is receiving the news that this country, which was created for dignity, is yet humiliated; that this country, which was created for security, is yet afraid; that this country, which was created for freedom, is yet subjugated; and that this country, which was created for good health, is yet ailing, with cholera assaulting its cities and villages whenever and however it wishes!

Then I experienced that sentiment that caused me to bow my head to the ground, and to grow small—a great distressing sense of shame for this homeland that we thought had surpassed that stage, the stage of backward, ignorant countries whose people are assaulted by plagues. And what a plague! Cholera—which we had thought would not return after it had subjected Egypt and its people to such tragedy at the beginning of this century.

"Would that my poetry could express" my dismay at what Egypt has done. What have the Egyptians done? It is said that they have founded many schools and educational institutes this century, that they have spread modern civilization to the greatest possible extent. They have a parliament as other nations have parliaments, and they have organized ministries as other developed nations have organized ministries. They even have a ministry of health as others have ministries of health. They have a capital that surpasses the capitals of many of the developed nations and that is comparable to those of the great nations. It is admired by Parisians, Londoners, and New Yorkers when they visit it and live there. They have also reached levels of luxury that have been denied many of the developed nations these days, until their wealth, luxury, and indulgence in the pleasures of life are taken as examples all over of the world. All this is true, and we hear of it when we visit Paris and other great cities in Europe and America.

All this is true, but it is also true that a month ago the whole world received a brief but extremely significant item of news. It received the news that, in that same Egypt that the Khedive Isma'il longed to see as a part of Europe, cholera had arrived and stayed; that despite wanting to repulse it, it is unable to do so; and that it is now appealing to the civilized world to protect its children from its evils and from its ugly assault.

I had thought that this sentiment of shame was a manifestation of a vanity, pride, and exaltation of oneself and one's nation. But as soon as I arrived in Egypt, I realized that I was not alone among cultured Egyptians in suffering from this kind of vanity, pride, and exaltation. For every cultured Egyptian appreciates himself and his country and recalls the efforts exerted by Egyptians in the recent past to elevate their nation to the levels of dignity, security, freedom, and health in body, heart, and mind it should occupy. Every cultured Egyptian is experiencing the same bitterness that I experienced—a mixture of unbearable sorrow and shame that bows our heads.

The passengers around me, Egyptian and foreign, look at me and are alarmed by the deep melancholy into which I have totally sunk. They keep their private suspicions to themselves. But some of them, trying to ease my distress and to reassure me, ask, "What do you think?"

I go no further than to remind them that I am acquainted with cholera and that I have mentioned it in some of my books that they have read, that I had witnessed this plague when I was no more than ten years old, and that it has left in my heart, and throughout my life, the greatest, most intense, most profound, most abominable scar.* For when children are affected by so profound and abominable an impression, they are never rid of it all their lives.

Did they believe me? I do not know—but I did not believe myself. For there was not the slightest connection, at that time, between the melancholy into which I had sunk and those memories of childhood, despite the bitterness and the grief they aroused in the soul. Rather it was born of that sentiment of sorrow and shame experienced by the cultured Egyptian when he sees his dreams, accomplishments, and endeavors—and those of many of his compatriots—collapsing as though they had never basked in those dreams, felt the pleasure of their accomplishments, or enjoyed their endeavors. It was as though they had not told themselves and each other that their distant dreams were beginning to draw nearer until they were on the verge of being realized, that their hard-won accomplishments were beginning to bear fruit, that their strenuous endeavors were beginning to bring them closer to their goal, that they would soon be able to rest, and that they would soon realize they had not spent their lives in vain or exerted their efforts to no avail. It was as though they had not told themselves and each other that they had inherited from their fathers a weary, tired, and ailing homeland and had stood by it until they had rebuilt some of its strength, health, stamina, and energy and had carried it long strides on the road to dignity and pride. It was as though they had not told themselves and each other that they could now hand it over to their children reassured that they had righteously upheld justice and valiantly performed their duty.

This sentiment of disappointment and the failure of one's efforts was the source of the melancholy in which I was sunk. But I could not speak of any of this to those around me. For they were too preoccupied with themselves to be

---

* Taha Hussein lost his favorite brother in that plague.

concerned with the cultured Egyptians and their aspirations, accomplishments, and endeavors, or with that desperate philosophy that flooded our hearts in those dismal days. They were discussing the various measures of protection and precaution they should adopt. In any event, they had realized that I did not like to listen to or participate in discussions on cholera, so they excused me. But the news did not excuse me. The ship's bulletin advised us each day of the number and location of casualties.

As we approached Alexandria, the passengers had no other topic of discussion. I had thought that when I arrived in Egypt I would find widespread melancholy, sorrow, and a general sense of shame as I myself was experiencing them.

But I arrive in Alexandria, and meet those Egyptians whom God wishes me to meet, and find that their lives are proceeding in the usual manner and that, although the plague frightens them, it does not turn them away from themselves or their pleasures. I find that the political developments sadden them, but do not distract them from themselves and their pleasures. I find that economic developments alarm them, but do not preoccupy them at the expense of themselves and their pleasures.

I arrive in Cairo and find what I had found in Alexandria. Those who are distracted from themselves and their pleasures by the plague and by the political and economic developments are a tiny minority. Apart from them, everyone else is proceeding with his life in the customary manner: wagging tongues and numb minds and hearts as hard as rocks, nay harder.

I cannot resist reciting the words of God Almighty:

> And when We would destroy a township We send commandment to its folk who live at ease, and afterward they commit abomination therein, and so the Word (of doom) hath effect for it, and We annihilate it with complete annihilation. (*XVII, 16*)

And:

> Allah coineth a similitude: a township that dwelt
> secure and well content, its provision coming to it
> in abundance from every side, but it disbelieved in
> Allah's favors, so Allah made it experience the
> garb of dearth and fear because of what they used
> to do. (*XVI, 112*)

The Feast approaches to find the affluent complacent,
not sensing that hundreds of families, in hundreds of cities
and villages, had been awaiting the feast as they had been,
longing for it even more than they had been. But the Feast
has broken its appointment with them and sent them death
in its stead, and along with death it has also sent them
woes and tears, chronic hardship, and endless misery.

Yes! Nor do they sense that their mother Egypt is ailing,
and that her ailment is terminal hemorrhage. But she is not
hemorrhaging blood. She is hemorrhaging her sons and
daughters. They sense none of this, or they sense it but do
not heed it, or they sense it and heed it but care and fear
only for themselves. As though they could live, luxuriate,
and enjoy life when sorrow, misery, and death pound their
blows on this miserable, unhappy nation.

Woe! Woe! This is only appeasing the soul with hope-
less wishes and deceiving it with false hopes. Egyptians
have two choices only: either they go on with their customary lives, caring only for themselves and their pleasures and interests, in which case let them rest assured that
this will bring an overriding and overpowering catastrophe
that neither spares nor forewarns; or they may adopt a new
life similar to the one they knew in the aftermath of the
First World War, based on unity, cooperation and the
eradication of the distances between the strong and the
weak, between the rich and the poor, between the healthy
and the ailing, in which case Egypt will withstand misfortune until it passes away, catastrophe until it is erased, and
agony until it subsides.

Which of the two roads do the affluent Egyptians wish to pursue? The road to death or the road to life?

It is a question I put to myself when I awake and when I go to sleep, beseeching God, in the interim, to spare me from despair and guard me from despondency, for:

Lo! None despaireth of the Spirit of Allah save disbelieving folk. (*XII, 87*)